Sherlock Holmes & The Case of the Poisoned Lilly

From The Notes of
John H. Watson M.D.

Edited by
Roger Riccard

First published in 2012 by
The Irregular Special Press
for Baker Street Studios Ltd
Endeavour House
170 Woodland Road, Sawston
Cambridge, CB22 3DX, UK

ISBN: 1-901091-52-X (10 digit)
ISBN: 978-1-901091-52-6 (13 digit)

Cover Concept: Antony J. Richards

Cover Illustration:

Typeset in 8/11/20pt Palatino

About the Author

Roger Riccard's family history has Scottish roots, which trace his lineage back to the Roses of Kilravock Castle near the village of Croy in Highland, Scotland. This British Isles ancestry encouraged his interest in the writings of Sir Arthur Conan Doyle at an early age. He has now taken pen in hand, (so much more poetic than 'sat down at his keyboard') to compose his own foray into the world of Sherlock Holmes.

Having earned Bachelor of Arts Degrees in both Journalism and History from California State University, Northridge, his career has progressed from teaching into business, where he has used his writing skills in various aspects of employee communications. He has also contributed to newspapers and magazines and has earned some awards for his efforts.

He currently lives in a suburb of Los Angeles, California with his wife, Rosilyn and their Chocolate Labrador Retriever, Tootsie Roll.

Preface

Having read numerous Sherlock Holmes novels and collections of short stories, I have come to the conclusion that Dr. Watson may have been even more disorganized than his celebrated friend.

While Watson tells us of the apparent disarray of Holmes's sitting room, the detective, at least, could find what he was looking for quickly. Our good doctor, on the other hand, seems to have scattered his notes and manuscripts among a variety of friends and relations; in attics, basements, trunks, boxes and briefcases, as well as the famous tin dispatch box in the vaults of the bank at Cox and Co., at Charing Cross.

I could easily add to this mélange by revealing that my late grandmother's maiden name was Ruby Hudson of Sanborn, New York. To acknowledge that she was also the niece of one Martha Hudson of London ... well, you, dear reader, could then draw your own conclusions as to how I came into possession of the notes and manuscripts used to put together this work.

My enthusiasm for the adventures of Sherlock Holmes has led me to collect many books of stories, pastiches and reference works regarding the great detective. With these as a foundation, I have attempted to strive for historic and geographic accuracy, as well as remain true to Watson's original language and tone. I hope that I have given these new tales the authentic timbre they deserve. However, there may be some instances where Victorian English terms would be too unfamiliar and distracting to the flow of the plot, and I have attempted to adjust for such language.

I hope that you will enjoy these works as my homage to Watson's originals, and find resumed appreciation for the world's finest private consulting detective.

Roger Riccard
Los Angeles
California
U.S.A.

To My Rosilyn.
My Angel, Partner, Coach and Love
Always

To Edward Hardwicke

Whose interpretation of the role of Dr. John H. Watson in the Granada Productions of *Sherlock Holmes*, has been an inspiration and guide in this expression of the Great Detective's adventures.

Chapter One

During the spring of 1890, there was one of those unusual occurrences in London. The bright blue sky above the city buildings gave the impression of hope for a beautiful day. The fog had dissipated early and the smoke of the city, with its yellow-grey hue, had not as yet choked the promise of the season. It was on this day that there began one of the most singular adventures which my friend, Sherlock Holmes, had ever the occasion to investigate.

I use the term 'singular' advisedly, as it was a many-faceted case with a duality to it that one would not dare to imagine.

It all began when my wife received the following correspondence:

> *My Dear Mary,*
>
> *You cannot possibly imagine my surprise when I read of your most unusual adventure in Lippincott's Magazine in your husband's story, 'The Sign of the Four'. I must congratulate you on your marriage and your success at having unravelled this mystery regarding the fortunes and fate of your unfortunate father.*

I would suppose that you also are surprised to hear from your old fellow-boarder from years past, whom you knew as Lillian Fields.

You are likely unaware that your former roommate is now parading about the stages of London under the name 'Loraine Fontaine'. (I simply could not imagine what the critics would have done had I used my real name. 'Lilly Fields' was an old joke that I had long ago tired of.)

I am afraid I may be imposing terribly upon an old friendship, but when I read your story it seemed a godsend, for I am at my wits end and it may be that the good Doctor's celebrated friend, Sherlock Holmes, is the only chance I have for peace of mind.

If only you might use your influence to convince him of the sincerity of my predicament I would be ever so grateful. As you may remember, I was blessed with an active imagination, which has helped me tremendously in my theatrical career. It was always controlled, and never distorted reality. So, when I tell you that I have been the victim of several 'coincidental' accidents lately, of such a nature that any of them might have ended my career, I am not succumbing to flattery of self-conceit.

I have a terrible foreboding and I feel I must relate my fears to Mr. Holmes. If you are of a mind to help an old friend, I will leave three passes for you at the Lyceum Theatre for this Saturday night and will meet you in my dressing room after the performance. I feel I must explain myself to Mr. Holmes in the setting where most of these events occurred, so that his investigation might be stimulated forthwith. I shall be ever so grateful, my dear Mary.

God bless you.
Loraine Fontaine

"John, we must see Mr. Holmes," Mary said. "Lilly is a dear old friend, even though we've lost track of each other over the years. The girl I remember is not given to fancy. If she believes she is in some trouble, then we must help her."

"Of course, my dear," I replied. "We shall go see Holmes at once." And with that we immediately set out for Baker Street.

Procuring a cab, we wound our way east from Kensington and northward into Baker Street. Upon our arrival, my former landlady, Mrs. Hudson, greeted us warmly and told us to go right on up, as Mr. Holmes was not engaged with anyone at present. Just as I crossed the landing and was about to knock, a familiar voice rang out, "Come in, Watson, and allow me to clear a chair for Mrs. Watson, as well."

I opened the door and stared at my old friend in astonishment. "Holmes, how could you have possibly known it was me and that I had brought Mary?"

"Come, come, old friend. Did you not think I would recognize your tread upon the stairs, which I have heard countless times? Then there were the lighter footfalls with you suggesting a woman, especially when the rustling of skirts became clear as you approached. I could only assume that you were accompanied by your wife, or were bringing me a new client. My choice was ultimately decided by one simple fact."

"And what would that be, Mr. Holmes?" asked Mary.

With a gesture of his long lean arm Holmes waved nonchalantly toward the window and replied, "I saw you disembark when your cab arrived."

I chuckled, but Mary, preoccupied with her friend's plight, gave in to a slight frown.

"Sometimes the simplest explanations are best," he said. "But obviously you have come upon a matter of some importance, as your wife's countenance clearly shows. Please, forgive me, take off your coats and pray tell me what problem brings you once again into my sitting room."

Mary handed Holmes the letter from Miss Fontaine. He examined the envelope first, as was his method. Proclaiming quietly, "Loraine Fontaine, humph, not her real name. Fair quality paper, modest ink, postmarked yesterday, smudge of makeup along the edge." He paused and sniffed it. "Theatrical makeup. She is an actress?"

Mary nodded and he continued, "Slightly indented as if she held it tightly and tapped it to her chin hesitantly before going through with her decision to post it to you."

He then proceeded to open it and continued his perusal. "She is right handed, about thirty, artistic of course, deeply troubled, appears to have a health problem. Probably unmarried, with no close male relatives to whom she can confide."

Mary was taken aback, "That is amazing, Mr. Holmes. I confess that I can confirm some of what you say, but I am completely at a loss as to your other deductions."

"Indeed, Holmes" I cried. "How can you tell from that letter that she has a health problem?"

"I have made a study of the science of graphology, Doctor. If you recall I used it somewhat in your wife's case, which you duly recorded in your fancifully titled story of *The Sign of the Four*. It is a fascinating subject and as a medical man you would appreciate its values. However, the analysis of handwriting is a discussion for another time. For now, I need to garner as many facts as I can before I meet this troubled woman tomorrow. Mrs. Watson, please tell me all you remember of your friend."

"Then you will help her, Mr. Holmes?" Mary answered. "I shall be ever so grateful."

"My good woman," said Holmes reaching out in that tender fashion he reserves for putting the fair sex at ease, patting my Mary's hand. "Watson knows that I would refuse him nothing and that would certainly apply to any request from the lady he obviously adores."

I smiled and Mary blushed slightly, then cleared her throat and began a reminiscence of Miss Lillian Fields.

"We were roommates for some months, while I was residing at the Percival Street Boarding House for Women after my father's disappearance. I was seventeen and she a year older. You are well aware of my circumstances, Mr. Holmes. In her case, she had come to board immediately

14

upon receiving an inheritance from her father's estate on her eighteenth birthday.

"Apparently, her mother had remarried a mere eight months after her father's death, when Lilly was sixteen. Her stepfather had, on occasion, made improper advances toward her."

"The scoundrel!" I exclaimed. "Could her mother not protect her?"

"Complaints to her mother went unheeded and disbelieved. Within a year her mother had borne another child, this time a son, whom the stepfather doted on. Lilly felt like an unwelcome stranger in her own home. Her inheritance had amounted to some three or four hundred pounds I believe. There is also a modest income from some business or property. I am sorry, Mr. Holmes, the details of her situation were really none of my concern. My memory of them may not be as clear as you would wish."

"That is quite all right," Holmes replied in all sincerity. "As I told you upon your first visit to these rooms, you are a model client with an excellent grasp for correct intuition. Please go on."

"Very well. Percival's was quite full at the time, as it had an excellent reputation and reasonable rates. But Lilly had her heart set upon it, for it was near the theatre district and she was of a mind to explore the performing arts. Upon her imploring the landlady, the situation was brought to me to see if I would consent to share my rooms.

"I was willing to do so, on a trial basis, and we hit it off quite well. She is much more, shall I say *flamboyant*, than I. Though we seemed to complement each other well and became fast friends."

"Tell me of her habits," Holmes requested "and her personality as it was when you knew her."

"Actually, as I think upon it, Mr. Holmes, the relationship we had reminds me of that which you and John enjoyed, when he shared these rooms with you prior to our marriage."

"How is that, my Love?" I interjected. I was very interested to hear how someone other than myself might perceive Holmes.

She looked up at me and, smiling, took my hand. Partially out of tenderness and in part, I believe, to gain strength to tell Holmes the bare facts.

"She was a very focused person. Once her mind was set upon something it would be nearly impossible to change the subject. Yet she could balance several things going on in her life at once. Much as you must handle numerous cases simultaneously.

"She was a voracious reader, primarily of classic literature and popular fiction. Anything that would help her to learn her chosen craft of acting she would devour.

"She was also, if you will forgive me, sir, not a tidy person. It was the one sore point between us. Books, magazines, costumes, wigs and makeup tended to multiply throughout our sitting room. But she could find the one thing she wanted in an instant, and was very careful about those things she considered precious to her."

"Ah," declared Holmes, "now what might those things have been?"

"She kept most of these items in her hope chest and was quite particular about that aspect of her privacy, which I naturally respected. She did have her father's silver watch and chain, which were of particular importance to her. In fact, and I only tell you this, Mr. Holmes, because I am aware that even the slightest trivialities can be of assistance to your investigations, she would actually sleep with it. She said it reminded her of her childhood when she would lay her head in her father's lap, hear the ticking through his waistcoat pocket and fall to sleep in his arms.

"She also had a keepsake that belonged to a great uncle, if memory serves. It was also silver on a silver chain and was a Saint Genesius medallion."

At this point, Holmes gestured toward me and pointed toward the bookcase where he kept his many reference volumes. Instinctively I knew he was asking me to look up this little known saint as he continued listening to Mary's narrative.

My wife's eye caught the act however, and immediately discerning its meaning explained to him, "Saint Genesius is the patron saint of actors, Mr. Holmes. Apparently this uncle was of the theatrical profession and an inspiration to her choice of career. Although not Catholic, he wore it as a good luck charm and passed it on to her. She wore it whenever her costume would allow, and would hang it from a hook on her grooming mirror when it would not."

"Thank you," he nodded, "anything further?"

"She kept odd hours due to her work. She ate sparingly, would never touch wine nor spirits. She had few gentlemen callers. Her experience with her stepfather and determination to become an actress would not let her contemplate the thought of marriage at that stage of her life.

"Let me think. Hmmm, she was a light sleeper. She would always dress impeccably well when leaving the house, in case she should come across someone who might be of an interest in helping her career."

"How was her career at the time you knew her?" asked Holmes.

"She was still in the learning stages. Rather like an apprentice, I suppose. She would attend lessons for diction, voice projection and singing as well as stage presence and bodily movements to help translate her character's emotions.

"I thought she was quite good at it, Mr. Holmes. However, at the time I left to become governess for Mrs. Forrester, she had yet to perform in any specific role. She was always cast as a member of a crowd or chorus of singers in the background."

"You say there were no men in her life. You are quite sure on that point?"

"Yes. As I said, she had occasional callers but she encouraged none of them and was never engaged. There was one fellow who was quite persistent for a time. A sailor, or merchant seaman, I believe. He would bring her flowers constantly and send her notes of rather rudimentary but, I am sure, heartfelt poetry. However, it was not serious and the last I knew, the relationship had ceased when his ship sailed on its next voyage."

Holmes steepled his fingers and sat back in his chair. "Interesting. Do you remember the name of this aspiring Romeo?"

"I am afraid I cannot immediately recall it, Mr. Holmes."

I leaned forward on the back of Mary's chair and questioned my friend. "Do you really think it important, Holmes? We are speaking of events that occurred over a decade ago."

"It is probably nothing, Watson, but in my experience it often pays not to discount emotions of the heart too quickly, no matter how old. Now, Mrs. Watson, is there any more upon which you may enlighten me as to this lady's past?"

"Not at the moment, Mr. Holmes. Rest assured I will confer upon you any further recollection should it come to mind."

"Then I thank you both for bringing me this pretty little problem. I shall meet you in front of the theatre tomorrow night at 7:15. If you would, please, drop this at the telegraph office on your way, Watson." Holmes stood, and quickly scribbled out a message reading:

Loraine Fontaine c/o Lyceum Theatre. - John and I shall attend with a friend. Please leave 3 passes under the name 'Morstan' - Sincerely, Mary

---

As I read the note Holmes seemed to read the question in my mind and said, "In case the lady's troubles originate within the theatre ranks it may be best our presence would be unknown until the proper time."

"Quite so, Holmes, until tomorrow then!" I helped Mary into her coat and we departed for home.

As we waited at the curb for a passing cab, Mary took my arm and looked me in the eye. "John, do you suppose I offended Mr. Holmes with my implication about his untidiness? I certainly did not mean to."

"Mary, my Love," I replied "Holmes takes no offence at truth. The only time I have seen him become insulted is when someone, in ignorance, compares him to the official police. I can assure you that he will now either ponder your friend's case over his pipe, or dismiss it completely from his mind until our meeting with Miss Fontaine, where more data will be forthcoming."

Chapter Two

The next day, being Saturday, passed quickly enough for me as an intermittent stream of patients passed through my consulting rooms. Since their complaints were primarily minor ailments, I was not unduly overtaxed and was eager to join my friend in his investigation.

Mary, on the other hand, was quite busily going through old trunks and boxes that might contain memorabilia of her youthful days at Percival's. She hoped to see if something should trigger a memory that would be helpful to Holmes in regards to Miss Fontaine.

At 6:00 p.m., we dined and I questioned my good wife about her quest.

"I am afraid I have found nothing useful, John," she replied. "Although there was something about that seaman that was very ... how shall I put it, un-sea like? A hobby or interest of some sort, that one would not expect of someone who spends his time traversing the oceans. I just can't put my finger on it yet."

"Well, my Sweet" I said, as I pursued the devouring of a mutton chop, "perhaps when you see Miss Fontaine tonight it will come back to you."

The June night was comfortable as we wound our way in a cab through the streets of London. Mary was ravishing in her modest yet elegant mauve gown with her white fur-lined cape. My own evening clothes were none the worse for wear, but next to her I felt like mere window dressing. Nearly a decade her senior, I still marvel at my good fortune in marriage to this young, beautiful and vibrant woman.

Shortly past 7:00 p.m., we found ourselves alighting at the Lyceum Theatre and crossing the pavement. I confess to a feeling of *déjà vu* when we reached the marble columns that fronted the entrance. For it was on this very spot, only two years past, that Holmes and I escorted Mary on her quest for her father's fate and to solve the mystery of her mysterious correspondent. That stranger had indulged her with annual pearls and then requested a face-to-face meeting, which prompted Mary to seek our assistance.

As we started across the pavement Mary gave me a nudge and let go of my hand, waving me forward. She kept going toward the entrance but had veered off to round the nearby column on the other side. Suddenly, Holmes emerged from behind the very column where we had been confronted on that fateful night. Upon stepping into my path he flinched visibly. I admit that I, too, jumped inwardly and began to raise my silver-headed cane at this sudden appearance.

Seemingly confused, Holmes looked behind me and then turned around to find my Mary, leaning against the column he had vacated, with her arms crossed.

"My dear Mr. Holmes, you must be more cautious when planning your little surprises. I observed you retreat behind this pillar when we were still twenty yards away."

Holmes chuckled and replied, "You, Mrs. Watson, are indeed a remarkable client. Watson, if you would be so good as to retrieve our tickets, I should like to make a study of the interior before they dim the gaslights."

Mary again took my arm, giving our friend a nodding smile and we continued to the box office. Securing our passes we entered the building. Holmes moved slowly through the foyer after we checked our hats and coats. He was no doubt, noting exits, stairwells, doorways and the like. When satisfied, he led the way into the theatre. Again he strolled casually, down to the orchestral stalls, eyes darting this way and that, until we reached our seats in the front row. Miss Fontaine had arranged for us to be just to the right, or stage left, of the orchestra pit. It appeared to be an excellent point for observing the performance and even allowed a small view of off-stage right, of which Holmes took advantage, having me sit in first, followed by Mary, then he on the aisle.

The theatre filled up quickly. Precisely at 7:30, the gas jets for the house lights were lowered and the footlights turned up. The orchestra began a lively overture as the curtain rose.

All in all it was an amusing performance and I am afraid I found myself so caught up in the enjoyment of it that I may not have been as observant as I should have been. Early on Mary pointed out her friend. Miss Fontaine was an attractive woman, if not a classic beauty. She was well-suited to this particular role where, through a comedy of errors and lucky circumstances, she ascended from a innkeeper's daughter and singer to a famous concert hall vocalist.

During the *entr'acte*, we stretched our legs with a leisurely walk to the lobby. Mary excused herself to the powder room and Holmes drew me into a quiet corner for discussion.

"Well, Watson, have you formed any opinion of our client?" he asked.

"She seems a fine actress. Her singing voice is remarkable in its variety and she seems to easily slip in and out of the various roles she must play during her character's stages of maturity. I thought her makeup was very well done in that she was able to look fifteen at the beginning of the play and now carries off twenty-five quite well, even though we know for a fact that she is thirty."

"What of her manner, Watson? Any conclusions there?"

"She seems very well at ease. As if she had been born to the stage. I detected no nervousness at all."

"Ah, yes. On stage she is a capable actress. However, I could see her in the wings and noted that she was very apprehensive. She was constantly looking about, as if attempting to sense impending danger. When her cues came it was as if a veil lifted from her the moment she stepped on stage, but off-stage was quite another matter. And what of other members of the cast – have you formed any opinions or observed anything noteworthy?"

"I cannot say that I took any particular notice of them, Holmes. I had concentrated my study on Miss Fontaine."

"Of course, good old Watson, always steady on course to the main objective. But I find that it is also wise to familiarize oneself with all the possible players in a game. I especially detected something in the young lady who plays her childhood friend and later becomes her maidservant."

I looked at my programme and took note of the woman's name. "You mean Miss Lily Harley?"

"Yes indeed. She is a fair actress with a well-trained voice. But note in your program that she is also Miss Fontaine's understudy."

"You have suspicions?"

"You know me better than that, Watson. It is much too early for suspicions without data. However, I did observe one or two things about her that may bear watching, should the facts lead in certain directions."

At this point Mary re-joined us and noted, "It has been a most delightful play and Lilly is performing marvellously, yet I noted she seemed pre-occupied while she was off-stage. What do you think, Mr. Holmes?"

Holmes looked at me with a cocked eyebrow and tilt of the head. With that quick half-smile of his that vanishes almost as quickly as it comes he turned to Mary. "I repeat, Mrs. Watson, you have an excellent intuition and refreshing powers of observation for your gender. Shall we return to our seats? I am anxious to see more of this little drama."

As we returned down the aisle I noticed this time that Miss Fontaine was in the wings and was waving at us with what seemed a relieved smile on her face. Mary smiled back and made a small wave of acknowledgement to her as we settled into our chairs just as the lights were dimmed.

The play continued and was delightfully humorous. The finale was met with a lengthy round of applause. Miss Fontaine came out for a final curtain call, during which a gentleman came from back stage and delivered to her a large bouquet of red roses. These were made all the more striking by the placement of a contrasting snow-white lily in the midst of the arrangement. A shadow briefly altered the actress' face, but she immediately regained her composure and curtsied gracefully to the audience. As the curtain fell upon this scene, Mary laid her hand upon my arm. "That's it, John! That was the sailor's hobby. He always personally arranged the flowers he brought to Lilly."

"You are quite sure?" asked Holmes.

"Oh yes, Mr. Holmes. I remember it now because he was so very creative at his mixture of flowers. Just like that one, with the lily mixed in with the roses."

"I see," said Holmes, nodding to himself. Suddenly he stood. "We must see your friend immediately. This way!"

Holmes led us to a curtained doorway at stage left. Behind the curtain was a slight incline leading up to stage level. We made our way through stored scenery and props and found a stagehand who pointed the way to Miss Fontaine's dressing room.

Upon our arrival, we knocked and the door was opened by a young coloured maiden. Miss Fontaine was seated at her dressing table, still in costume, contemplating the flower arrangement in her hand. She gave a quick start when Holmes introduced himself from the doorway, followed by a brief cry of pain from what appeared to be an encounter with a rose thorn. She placed the roses in a vase then, pressing the wound to her lips to stop the bleeding, she turned and greeted us warmly.

"Mr. Holmes, thank God you've come. Mary, my old friend, I cannot thank you enough." At which point she gave Mary a long hug. "And this must be your husband, Dr. Watson."

I took the offered hand and bowed. "A pleasure to meet you, Miss Fontaine. Mr. Holmes has expressed an interest in your case and we are all very anxious to learn what concerns you so."

"Yes please, sit down all of you."

"Thank you," replied Holmes "Please, tell me your predicament. I assume the floral arrangement you just received is the newest piece to your puzzling troubles."

"Why, yes, Mr. Holmes."

"Your expression was quite obvious, both upon your receipt of them and just now during your contemplation. Have you received such a bouquet before?"

"Yes. This is the third Saturday in a row that I have received exactly such flowers. Red roses, with a single white lily."

"Mrs. Watson tells me you once had a beau who was quite the floral arranger, though he was a seaman by trade."

The actress looked over at Mary with surprise written upon her face. "You mean ... My God I hadn't even thought of him. But that was over ten years ago!"

"Exactly who are we speaking of and what details can you recall?"

"Forgive me, Mr. Holmes. The gentleman in question is Gregory McAllister. He was a merchant seaman who happened to catch a show I was in when I was still beginning my career. Somehow, he picked me out of a chorus of girls and began calling upon me in hopes of a courtship. I went on outings with him a few times, dinner, the theatre, but it was all in fun. There was no romance involved. He never spoke of marriage. Poor boy, he didn't think he was good enough for me and I was not at a time of my life where I was encouraging anyone along those lines."

"But he sent you flowers?"

"Yes, Mr. Holmes, on several occasions, as Mary must have told you. But it was so long ago I did not make the connection. So many other things have been happening that seem to lead in a direction opposite of romance."

"Yet the fact that these arrangements contain a lily, suggest that they are from someone in your past who knows your true name. Mr. McAllister seems a prime candidate. There have been no cards or notes attached?"

"None, Mr. Holmes, it was all a puzzlement to me until now."

"Well, we shall have to see where that thread leads. You stated in your letter that you feared physical harm such as might be detrimental to your career. Would you please elaborate on the circumstances that caused you to seek my help?"

At that moment the young maid spoke up "Excuse me, Miss Lorraine," she intoned with just a hint of a southern American accent. "You haven't had your milk yet and you knows how your stomach gets. Would you like anything for your guests?"

"Oh, gracious yes, forgive me. Please bring in a teapot, Caroline." The young lady disappeared down the hall.

"Caroline is my dresser," noted our client "She is indispensable to me."

"I see," said Holmes. "Any other servants or assistants?"

"No, Mr. Holmes. Caroline is quite all I need. I've not succumbed to the conceit of a prima donna yet."

When the young lady returned with the tea service Miss Fontaine continued. "Caroline, I was about to relate to Mr. Holmes the mishaps that have befallen me lately. Would you please stay? You may be able to help me remember some details."

There was insufficient seating for us all and so I rose and gave Caroline my chair while I stood behind Mary, who was seated next to the dressing table. Neither Holmes nor I indulged in the tea, but Mary poured herself a cup and added sugar and milk as was her custom. Our leading lady forsook the tea in favour of a glass of plain milk and as I took out my notebook, Miss Fontaine began her story.

"It all started not quite two months ago, Mr. Holmes. In fact the first incident took place at the final dress rehearsal for our current production. That would have been on Thursday, the 11th of April.

"We were getting ready to rehearse the second act when the backdrop curtain for that scene apparently stuck, only about a third of the way down. It was taking some time for the stagehands to repair and so Lionel, that's Lionel Ferguson our director, ordered everyone on stage to run through their parts anyway. We went on with the scene and all was going well when suddenly there was a cry of alarm and the curtain came crashing down. It brushed my shoulder and knocked me down. I was quite startled by it of course, but even as Lionel and the cast gathered around me, I knew I was not seriously injured.

"It seemed a mere accident, although I counted myself fortunate not to have taken the full brunt of the weight of all that material coming down in a heap. As I arose and was brushing myself off, a voice came from the back of the theatre. A deep, coldly penetrating voice, that I knew all too well.

"'Are you all right, Miss Fontaine?' he said. I knew in an instant it was Harrison Colby."

"The infamous producer of the more bawdy productions around London?" enquired Holmes. "You had made his acquaintance before?"

Miss Fontaine laughed sarcastically and coughed. "There isn't a moderately attractive female in all of London's thespian circles whose acquaintance Harry Colby hasn't made it his business to cultivate. Even more, whenever he could charm them with that silver tongue of his.

"I had the unpleasant experience of working for him briefly some six years ago in a production he called 'Queen of the Nile'. I was only with his show for a few days rehearsal, when I saw the shameless costumes and heard some of the other actresses speaking of the 'undress' rehearsals. I immediately gave notice and quit. He threatened to have me blackballed from the theatre, but I eventually found serious work. These past four years have been quite satisfying and rewarding.

"Unfortunately, since my recent rise in popularity, Harry occasionally comes around claiming I owe him a show and makes all kinds of legal threats, but Lionel assures me he has no claim on me."

"Was this his purpose for being at the theatre the day of your accident?" asked Holmes.

"I don't think so, Mr. Holmes." she paused and took another sip of her milk. "When Lionel heard his voice he turned like a man possessed and screamed "Get out of here you snake! How dare you set foot in a legitimate theatre? I'll not have you trying to entice any of my people away with your shallow promises or empty threats."

"'Have a care, sir', Colby said, pointing his cane at the stage. 'I have a great deal of influence among the theatres of London and I daresay I could stop this pretty little production of yours, if I should wish to waste my money to do so. My only purpose is to discuss the wire I sent you last week. Have you considered my proposal?'

"Well, Mr. Holmes," said our actress, "I have never seen Lionel lose his temper as he did at that moment. He grabbed a prop rifle from one of the actors playing a guardsman and brandished it like a club as he leaped down into the orchestra pit and screamed 'Never, you crook!'.

"Colby stood his ground for a moment, then replied in that deep condescending voice, barely above a whisper, that he uses when being deliberately irritating, 'Evidently this is not a convenient time. I shall return when you are in a more amenable mood.' Immediately he turned on his heel and strode out before Lionel could climb over the rail and up the aisle. Though, he did cry a warning after him, that if Colby ever came near him again he would kill him."

"Really?" responded Holmes, as he motioned for me to make a note of that. "And what was the result of the investigation of the curtain falling?"

"It was called an accident, Mr. Holmes. Apparently the pressure they put on the pulleys and ropes to loosen them was sufficient to snap one of the ropes at a weak spot and I happened to be in the path of the fall."

"But you are not convinced?" stated Holmes flatly.

"I would have been satisfied, Mr. Holmes, had that been the end of it, but soon more things began to happen. I was nearly run down by a runaway horse and wagon just a week later. A few days after that, Caroline noticed a strong smell coming from here in my dressing room while I was performing on stage."

The young servant spoke up at that point, "It was the gas, sir! They was a leak in the pipe and it done filled the room. Lucky we wasn't all blown up!"

"It was a terrible experience." Miss Fontaine continued. "My costumes were all in here and I had to finish the performance with that odour in my nostrils for over an hour. The audience that night must have thought me mad with my constant fanning of myself. I have felt ill from its effects ever since."

"And what was the cause of this leaky pipe?" asked my friend.

"Apparently, there had been some workman in the building running new pipe for additional lighting. It was assumed they had tapped off my line and failed to retighten the fittings properly."

"Surely such incompetence is not the mark of a true tradesman!" I exclaimed.

"Indeed not, Doctor." replied Holmes. "I believe it worth further inquiry ... Miss Fontaine! Are you ill?"

The actress had suddenly hunched over in her chair, one hand to her forehead, the other clutching the back of her chair as though she were hanging on for dear life.

"I ... feel dizzy." She whispered hoarsely. Then her fingers gave way and she fell, just as Holmes reached out to catch her and ease her to the floor.

"Water, quickly!" I said to young Caroline, and she ran out the door. I knelt beside the fallen actress and took up her wrist. After a few agonizing seconds I told Holmes, "Her pulse is racing like a runaway steam engine. Mary, fold that blanket and put it under her feet and hand me that coat."

Mary, with her usual efficiency, tossed me the coat and I draped it over Miss Fontaine's body, which had begun to shiver with minor convulsions. As I did so, Mary propped up her feet and removed her shoes. "Her feet are like ice, John."

I checked her pupils and found them contracted in her unconscious state. "Holmes, we must get her to St. Bartholomew's immediately, I can do nothing here."

At that moment, Caroline returned with the water and Holmes instructed her to call for a carriage to transport her mistress to the hospital.

"There's a wagon behind the theatre all hitched up, Mr. Holmes. They use it to run for supplies they might need in case something goes wrong during the show."

"Then we must bundle her off in it immediately! You, come help carry her!" ordered Holmes to a passing member of the troupe. Then to Mary he said, "Please go with them. You may be of some comfort when she regains consciousness."

The man and I carried the comatose actress to the alley behind the theatre. He took the reins as Mary and I tried to make Miss Fontaine comfortable on a pallet. We made haste with our patient, toward St. Bartholomew's Hospital. Holmes had chosen to remain behind and I now must relay what he subsequently reported to me.

Chapter Three

There was a significant amount of hubbub from the other actors and stagehands. Holmes ignored their questions and closed the door. He rubbed his hands together, eyes darting about the room. The St. Genesius medal was hanging in its prominent spot on the mirror, as Mary had described. All else seemed in order.

Settling finally on the milk glass, which had fallen to the floor during Miss Fontaine's faint, he bent and picked it up. It was cracked from its impact and the majority of its contents were spilled onto the floor and rapidly soaking into the wood and the napkin that had lain upon Miss Fontaine's lap. He smelled the milk, examined the glass with his lens and carefully set it down, where it had fallen with the napkin over the top of it.

Moving on to the roses, he again examined them closely and found the thorn which had drawn blood from Miss Fontaine's finger. He removed that particular stem and noted a small bit of greyish thread caught on another thorn, which he added to his collection.

Before he could continue his study, two men burst into the room. The first, very tall and lanky, with dark hair and moustache, looked to be in his middle thirties. This, it turned out, was the play's director, Lionel Ferguson.

"Who are you?" he demanded. "What has happened to Miss Fontaine?"

"She has taken quite ill, I'm afraid," answered Holmes. "She is being transported to St. Bartholomew's as we speak. Ah, Irving, would you please shut the door, so that we can discuss matters more discreetly?"

This last comment was addressed to the other gentleman, of nearly the same height as Holmes but a bit heavier and twenty years his senior. This was Henry Irving, well-known actor and the owner of the Lyceum. His face brightened in recognition of the famous detective.

"Mr. Sherlock Holmes!" he cried, and put out his hand to shake that of his old friend. "What's this about Loraine going to hospital? And what brings you here tonight?"

Holmes relayed what had occurred. Ferguson became exceedingly agitated and suddenly stood, proclaiming, "I must go to her!" and he quickly excused himself. As he opened the door and rushed out, Caroline stepped into the doorway and asked if she could come in and clean up. Holmes invited her to take a seat.

"Miss Caroline I must ask, with your permission sir," he nodded at Irving, "that absolutely nothing in this room is to be touched until I have finished my examination. And I am sure the police will want the same restriction as well, should my suspicions prove correct."

"The police?!" exclaimed Irving "You suspect this was a criminal act?"

"Miss Fontaine was engaging my professional services due to some untoward events that have plagued her recently," replied Holmes, steepling his fingers. "This sudden illness hardly seems to be coincidental."

After further examination of the items on the dressing table he then turned his attention to the servant girl.

"Miss Caroline, is it your mistress' usual custom to have milk after an evening performance?"

"Why no, Mister Holmes sir," she answered. "Usually Miss Loraine would have a glass of milk here in her dressing room *before* the show and then have dinner afterward. She said the milk helped her hunger pains since she couldn't bring herself to eat before she went on."

"Where is the milk kept?" enquired Holmes

Irving spoke up, "We've an icebox and pantry set up in one of the storage rooms. Loraine's milk would be in there."

"Show me," Holmes requested, springing to his feet.

The three of them quickly passed out into the hall, stopping only to lock the dressing room door against any intrusion.

Arriving at the icebox, Holmes retrieved the pitcher and found it half full.

"Did Miss Fontaine have any milk tonight before we saw her?"

"She had a glass before the show like always, Mister Holmes," said Caroline "I think this is the first time she also had a glass afterwards. Like I said, she usually goes out to dinner. The only milk missing are the two glasses I poured for her and what I put in the tea set and brought to the room."

"And everyone has access to this area?"

"Yes." replied Irving, "All the cast and crew are free to eat back here."

"I see." Holmes thought a moment, and then suddenly pulled paper and pencil from his pocket. He scribbled a quick message. He also dipped his handkerchief into the pitcher and rolled it up to keep the dry side out.

Handing these to the proprietor he said, "Irving, do you have a stagehand or someone you can trust to deliver this to Dr. Watson at St. Bartholomew's immediately? It could be a matter of life or death!"

"Aye Holmes, I'll take care of it straight away." He took the paper and cloth, gave it to a young lad sweeping the floor, and sent him off with money for a cab. Returning to Holmes he asked, "Is Miss Fontaine in danger?"

"Yes, Irving and more than she." Returning to the dressing room with the milk pitcher in hand he picked up the fallen glass with the few remaining drops.

"May I have a box to transport some of this milk and a few items from here? There's much work to be done."

He paused as the much-stressed theatre owner started to question him regarding our client's health. Holding up his hand he replied. "I cannot theorize without facts. However, it seems apparent that Miss Fontaine's understudy will have to take over her role for the time being. I shall keep you apprised of any developments."

*   *   *

While Holmes was conducting his investigation, Mary and I had seen to Miss Fontaine's comfort as best we could during the wagon ride. The driver was in such a rush, however, he made a wrong turn on a narrow street. It took several minutes to find our route again, as the wagon was too large to turn around on that road. She was pale and her breathing shallow. We used the travelling rugs under the wagon seat to keep her as warm as possible. When we alighted at Bart's, two attendants bustled her off to a room straight away. As we stepped into the hospital lobby out of the cool evening air however, Mary suddenly fell against me and I barely caught her before she dashed her head on the floor.

"Mary!" I cried, "What is it? What's wrong?" But she had fainted and could not reply. An orderly rushed over and helped me place her on a trolley and we rushed her down the hall into the room next door to where her friend now lay under examination by a Dr. Eckstein.

Eckstein apparently called to me as we passed by, but in my concern over Mary his plea fell on deaf ears. The fact that Mary had succumbed so soon after her friend made me suspect some common agent at work. But Mary's pulse was uncommonly slow, her pupils dilated. Symptoms just the opposite of those that felled the actress.

Eckstein came into the room and called my name again. "Watson, what do you have here? Is she suffering the same malady as the lady next door?"

"This is my wife, Mary. We were visiting your patient, Loraine Fontaine when Miss Fontaine became ill and we rushed her here. Mary just now fainted in the lobby but she is not exhibiting the same symptoms as her friend."

"May I?" asked Eckstein, as he moved to the bedside to examine Mary.

"Of course," I replied stepping aside and letting him repeat much the same routine I had just completed.

"Were they eating anything before the onset of these symptoms?" he enquired

"No," I replied. "Mary only took tea. Miss Fontaine just had milk."

"Hmm. Do me a favour would you, Watson? Please step next door and examine Miss Fontaine again. I'd like you to confirm what I found."

"What do you think it is, Doctor?"

"I'd rather not prejudice your judgment with my opinion as yet. Please take your time, while I arrange some tests for your wife."

It was only after I stepped into the hallway, out of sight of my beloved Mary, that I realized Eckstein had appealed to my medical professionalism to get me out of the room. This enabled him to conduct a more thorough examination that might prove awkward with a husband present. He was a slender man, and quite a bit shorter than I, young with blond hair and pale blue eyes confirming his Germanic name. We knew each other only casually as members of the medical profession, but I had heard he was an excellent diagnostician. Now I realized he was a fair psychologist, as well.

As I approached Miss Fontaine's room, a tall thin man came rushing into the hallway crying out, "Where's Loraine Fontaine?"

Unaware of his identity, and knowing she was suspicious of physical harm, I immediately approached the man and introduced myself.

"I am Dr. Watson. Who are you seeking sir?"

"Loraine Fontaine, the actress. Where is she?"

I took his arm and gently suggested, "Come with me to the front desk and we'll see what we can find."

He shook my hand off violently and in a raised voice replied "I've been to the front desk! They told me she would be in this corridor. Now where is she?"

"I must ask you to lower your voice, sir!" I said, raising my own in what I hoped was a commanding tone from my military days. "You'll disturb the other patients. Miss Fontaine is still being examined and you cannot see her yet. May I ask who you are, sir, and what is your connection to the lady?"

"I'm sorry, Doctor. I am Lionel Ferguson, the director of her play at the Lyceum theatre, and... a close friend. Please, can you tell me, is she all right?"

I motioned for him to have a seat with me at a bench in the hallway and explained that there were still tests being run and it could take some time before we knew anything.

"Can I see her?" he implored.

Still not convinced that he might not be involved in Miss Fontaine's precarious fate I put him off saying "I am afraid that would not be advisable. She is unconscious and must be protected from outside contact until we are sure what is wrong." Then, hoping to clarify his sincerity I added. "Have you been aware of any deliberate attempts to harm Miss Fontaine?"

He looked at me sharply and then asked "What did you say your name was, Doctor?"

"Dr. John Watson," I replied.

"I should have realized," he said. "Sherlock Holmes is even now examining Loraine's room. Yes, she must have told you about the curtain and the wagon and the gas. I must admit, up until the gas leak I thought it mere coincidence, but that incident seemed aimed deliberately at her. I contacted the police, but they've come up with nothing."

At that moment there was a commotion down the hall. I stood and saw a young lad arguing with a nurse. "This 'ere message is for Dr. Watson!" he cried "I got to deliver it meself!"

I called down the hall "It's all right, nurse, let him come, I'm Dr. Watson." The boy rushed to me and handed me the note clutched in his hand and a handkerchief which I recognized as Holmes'. "It's from Mr. 'Olmes, sir. 'E says it's a matter o' life or death! 'Ello, Mr. Ferguson, sir."

"Hello, Drew," replied Ferguson, standing as well and trying to see over my shoulder "What is it, Doctor?"

I took the note from the lad and read as follows:

> *See to your wife, Watson. Suspect poison in milk. Type unknown. Returning to Baker St. to ascertain. Meet me soonest.*
>
> *Holmes*

"Eckstein!" I cried, turning to find that he, too, had stepped into the hallway at the sound of the commotion.

"What is it, Watson?" he asked

"I've just received this note from Sherlock Holmes. He suspects poison."

"Poison?" cried Ferguson, sinking back onto the bench.

"Ah ha!" replied the young physician, "That coincides with my diagnoses of both ladies. Does he say what kind of poison?"

"No," I replied. "Only that he thinks it was in the milk and he sent along this sample." And I handed him the milk-soaked handkerchief.

"Very well, I will order her stomach pumped immediately!" He turned and spoke to a nurse who rushed off to retrieve the necessary equipment.

I then felt a tug at my sleeve. It was the young messenger.

"'Scuse me sir, did I do all right? Was I in time?"

"You did well, lad." I assured him "What's your name?"

"Drew, sir. I work at the theatre."

"Well, Drew," I said, "You did very well indeed. Here take this for your trouble and cab fare back to the theatre." I reached into my pocket and realized I had no small coinage with me so picked out a half-crown and pressed it into his hand.

"Oh no, sir, it's too much!"

"Nonsense, lad!" I admonished him. "You may well have saved a person's life tonight." I hesitated as I looked into that eager face. The boy couldn't have been more than ten years old or so. He was dressed in dusty clothes that were a bit large for his stature, as evidenced by rolled up sleeves and trouser cuffs. He reminded me of Holmes' Baker Street Irregulars and the thought struck me that I could apply one of Holmes methods in this case.

"If you feel a desire to perform further service to merit your reward, you keep an eye out at the theatre for any suspicious characters, or anyone doing anything out of the ordinary. Then you contact me, or Mr. Holmes, at 221 B Baker Street. Have you got that, Drew?"

He looked down at the money in his hand and beamed, "Yes, sir, Dr. Watson! Ye can count on me, sir!"

"There's a good lad. Off with you now and keep an eye out!"

"Aye, sir, sharp as an 'awk. Goodbye, sir, and thank ye!" He turned and rushed off clutching his well-deserved prize.

Chapter Four

Leaving Ferguson on the bench in silent contemplation, I went back into Mary's room and took her hand in mine and soothed her hair. Knowing that a person unconscious could often hear, though not react, I spoke softly assuring her that all would be well.

Hearing a sound in the doorway, I turned and saw Ferguson standing there. "Your wife was poisoned as well, Doctor?" He asked. I nodded.

"Who would do such a thing? How could they? Who could harm such a lovely creature as Loraine?"

The nurse and doctor then returned with the equipment necessary to treat Mary and Eckstein asked us to wait in the hall.

Knowing I could do nothing more until the procedure was over I turned my attention to Ferguson. "If you will forgive me, sir, your reaction seems to indicate something more than an employer's concern. What, if I may ask, is your relationship to Miss Fontaine?"

He looked up like a man who had all the wind taken out of his sails. Gone was the demanding director as he said, "I believe your reputation, and Holmes', allows me to take you into my confidence, Doctor. I admit I have come to have strong feelings for Loraine."

"Was she aware of your attraction?" I asked.

"I have not expressed myself to her as yet. I was waiting until the show finished its run at the end of summer, when we would not have the 'director-actress' relationship to complicate matters. Then I hoped to make my feelings known and begin a courtship."

"I see." Then, deciding in his favour, I stood and said, "Come with me."

I led him to Miss Fontaine's room where he rushed to her side as the nurse stepped back with my assurances.

I questioned the nurse as to Miss Fontaine's vital signs as he held her hand, much as I had done with Mary. There had been some slight change in that her pulse was slowing again, though still quite high. She also told me that the stomach pump would be brought in as soon as they were done with Mary.

This caused me some professional concern and I asked the nurse out into the hall so as not to be overheard by Ferguson.

"Why was Miss Fontaine not given treatment first?" I asked her. "She fell ill nearly half an hour before Mary. She may be in much more serious condition."

"I don't know, Doctor. I'm just following Dr. Eckstein's orders and monitoring her vital signs. He did administer some medication to Miss Fontaine before he went on to care for Mrs. Watson."

"What sort of medication?" I asked

"You'll have to ask him, sir. He has all his notes with him."

I dismissed her to return to Miss Fontaine and went back to waiting outside Mary's room.

By this time, Dr. Eckstein had completed his work and assured me that everything was under control. Well-trained staff members were seeing to Mary's every need and would call us if necessary.

Steering me in the direction of Miss Fontaine's room, he asked me my opinion of her illness.

As we walked, I decided to take Dr. Eckstein into my confidence. I told him that our actress friend had appealed to Holmes for help regarding several recent mishaps. I reiterated to him that she too, must be a poison victim. He nodded in agreement but reminded me that her symptoms were nearly polar opposite to those of Mary.

"Is that why you've pumped Mary's stomach but only given medication to Miss Fontaine?"

"Yes," he replied "Miss Fontaine's symptoms called for a general antidote to reduce her pulse rate. Her reaction to that treatment will determine if her stomach needs pumping as well."

"But they both drank the suspect milk." I replied

"Yes, but you said Mary had the milk in her tea. That combination could have drastically changed the reactivity to the poison. I'm still not convinced that Miss Fontaine's condition is caused by the same agent."

Continuing on he said, "Let us look at this mystery the way your celebrated friend would. How many people were in the room?"

"Five."

"And only these two women have exhibited any ailments?"

"Well, I cannot say for certain as I have not seen Holmes or Miss Fontaine's servant since we left the theatre, and Mary's symptoms did take time to manifest."

He raised a finger to make a point "But the note written by Mr. Holmes makes no mention of the servant falling ill, and he apparently is quite unharmed, so I believe we can rule out any airborne poisons for that should have affected all of you. That brings us to the milk. If the milk were the cause, then both women should be exhibiting the same symptoms, but they are obviously suffering from two very different maladies. Therefore, we would have to consider the tea as having a different type of poison from the milk, or that there is another poison at work that Miss Fontaine contracted in some other fashion."

"Yes, obviously," I agreed. "But it seems beyond all odds that there should be two different poisons present at the theatre."

"If, in fact, they were both poisoned," he countered. "Either may be suffering from some other illness, or it may be the effect of long term exposure to some toxin. Did Miss Fontaine mention any other symptoms at all before she fainted?"

I could not recall anything and told Eckstein so. (At the time I was preoccupied with Mary and had forgotten about Miss Fontaine's exposure to the gas and that she was still feeling its effects.)

"It may be something as simple as a spider bite or as sinister as a poisoned pin in her costume," he suggested, as we approached Fontaine's room.

"Wait!" I cried, "Check the middle finger of her right hand. She cried out in pain as she was putting roses into a vase a few minutes before she fainted. It may have been a rose thorn or a spider among the leaves."

As we entered her room, Ferguson looked up and I introduced him to Dr. Eckstein. He stepped back and Eckstein went to the actress and carefully examined her hand with a magnifier. "She does have a puncture wound here. I'll order a blood sample and see if there is any trace of poison. Then we'll know better how to treat her. In the meantime, Doctor, I suggest you make yourself comfortable until we have finished with Mrs. Watson. I'll let you know if there is any change."

I knew that sitting around twiddling my thumbs would do no good and would probably only cause a rise in my own blood pressure. I determined to do what I could toward the investigation of this apparent crime and take advantage of the hospital's library to study the possibilities. I found a pageboy and sent Holmes the following telegram:

> *Mary taken ill. Opposite symptoms of Fontaine. Will remain to determine conditions of both and research possible poisons. Will advise when results known.*
>
> *Watson*

Upon sending this off I then retired to the hospital library and began my researches.

It was nearly 2:00 a.m. when a hospital orderly aroused me from my concentrations on the medical books spread out before me.

"Excuse me, Dr. Watson?"

"Eh, oh yes?" I replied, somewhat groggily.

"Dr. Eckstein says your wife is better and should be coming round soon if you'd like to be there."

Immediately, I leapt to my feet and scrambled down the stairs, charging the young man to see that no one touched the books while I was gone.

Arriving at Mary's room I found Eckstein checking her pulse and making note of it in her file.

"Ah, there you are, Watson! Your wife is much better. She'll be a little weak and sore from the procedure, but her pulse is back up and her temperature is nearly normal. We seem to have caught it in time."

Just then, Mary began to stir and I rushed to her bedside. Taking her hand I leaned over and spoke softly.

"Mary, dearest, it's John."

She rolled her head toward my voice but couldn't seem to open her eyes.

"Mary, it's John. Open your eyes, Love."

With what seemed a great effort, she managed to open her left eye and after a moment, a glimmer of a smile turned up the corner of her lip. She opened her other eye and whispered hoarsely, "John, what ... what happened? Throat sore ..."

"Don't try to talk, my Love. You're at the hospital. You passed out from some type of poison and they've pumped your stomach. You're going to be all right."

Slowly she nodded and then she remembered, "Lilly?" she implored with a stricken look on her face.

Not wanting to upset her further I answered, "She's responding to medication and resting. The doctors are keeping a close eye on her."

In her still-recovering state she did not press me for any further details and indeed, it was just as well, since I had not been apprised of Miss Fontaine's condition in over two hours.

45

"She'll be all right now." Eckstein's voice whispered behind me as he put his hand on my shoulder. "We should let her rest, and you should get some sleep yourself, Watson."

I gently laid Mary's hand down, kissed her forehead and wished her a good sleep.

Eckstein and I walked quietly out into the hallway.

"I mean it, Watson, you look all done in. Mary will be fine now. She just needs a day or two's rest. We'll look after her."

Bleary eyed I looked at him and shook my head. "No, I've been doing research up in the hospital library. I've narrowed the possibilities down somewhat but..."

"We've analyzed the poison from the milk," he interrupted, "It explains your wife's symptoms perfectly, with her medical condition."

"What medical condition are you referring to?" I asked, "Her health has always been fine."

Eckstein gazed at me curiously, "She has a heart murmur. You didn't know?"

I stared back at him and admitted, "I've never had the occasion to medically examine her to any extent. She's never complained of anything that would lend itself to such a condition."

"Well, it may be something that is just beginning to manifest, or it may be a condition from birth that is growing more pronounced. You had better keep an eye on that."

Stunned, I answered. "Yes indeed, Doctor, of course."

Continuing his remarks he stated "What's puzzling us is Miss Fontaine. We know she had the same poison from the milk, but her symptoms don't correlate. The tests on her blood were inconclusive for anything else."

"Wait!" I declared. "I just remembered. She was exposed to a leaking gas line several weeks ago and said she was still feeling its effects. Yet that hardly seems possible to combine with a poison after so long."

Eckstein looked thoughtful as he rubbed the back of his neck.

"It fails to answer the cause of the opposite symptoms but it could explain why she was so susceptible, being in a weakened condition. I'll look into that. You, go home and get some rest. You're dead on your feet. This is my normal shift so I'm used to these hours. I'll check your books in the library and see what I can come up with. I'll leave all my notes with Dr. Kennedy, when he takes over in the morning"

Admitting he was right, I grudgingly agreed. He started to walk me to the door, paused and asked, "Didn't you have an overcoat, Doctor?"

I realized I was still in my evening clothes and my overcoat and hat had been checked back at the theatre. Just then a voice spoke up from behind us. "Here, Doctor you can take mine. I won't be leaving for awhile."

It was Ferguson. He had just come out into the hallway from Miss Fontaine's room and held out his overcoat for me.

"You should get some rest too, Mr. Ferguson." said Eckstein. "Miss Fontaine seems stable for now."

"Stable perhaps, but not yet conscious. If you don't mind, Doctor I'll stay."

"Very well. Now you, Watson, take his coat and be off. Mary will be just fine. I'll look into your research. But who knows? Maybe Mr. Holmes already has it worked out."

I did his bidding and donned Ferguson's coat. It was bit tight in the shoulders and waist so I could not button it but it was serviceable against the night chill, and a scarf in the pocket proved suitable for my neck and chest. Though hatless, I was somewhat protected and just as well, for it took some time to hail a cab at that time of the morning.

The lights of London had dimmed significantly by that hour and the stars shone bright in the cloudless spring sky. When I finally flagged down a drowsy driver with a drowsier dray mare, I found myself automatically answering his query for my destination with, "221B Baker Street."

Chapter Five

I must confess that I dozed off and was startled awake by the driver's announcement "Oi, sir! 221 Baker Street! Rise 'n shine!"

Momentarily confused that I was at my old lodgings instead of my home in Kensington I thought to admit my mistake to the driver and have him push on. However, I noted that the light in Holmes's study was still burning brightly and so I decided to report to him and learn whatever information he may have gleaned, as well. Numbly I paid the man and fished out the key that Mrs. Hudson had allowed me to keep, knowing that I would undoubtedly continue my work with Holmes.

Quietly I slipped the key into the lock and entered, being careful not to make any unnecessary noise and rouse our long-suffering landlady at this hour.

Tip-toeing my way up the stairs, I slowly opened the door to our old sitting room and found Holmes at his makeshift laboratory peering into a microscope.

"Ah, Watson, there you are." he murmured. "I trust your wife is on the road to recovery?"

"Indeed, Holmes," I replied. "Your message and sample put her doctor on the right track and she is resting comfortably. How did you know she was better?"

Looking up he continued, "I know you, my old friend. All the warriors in Afghanistan could not drag you from your wife if she were still in danger. What of Miss Fontaine? You said her symptoms were the opposite of Mary's. Have the doctors come to any conclusion?"

I told him of the blood tests that Eckstein had run and that she was somewhat responding to the general antidote he had administered. I also told him of my encounter with Ferguson and subsequent actions.

"I thought I recognized Ferguson's coat upon you. We shall return it and retrieve yours later today, if you are up to re-visit the Lyceum after some rest."

I nodded and yawned, "If I can be of service, Holmes, of course."

"Spoken like a true soldier. Now off to bed with you and I will finish up here. I believe I'm getting close to the solution to Miss Fontaine's malady."

"Really, Holmes?" I perked up slightly "What ..."

"No, no, Watson. I had prepared for a long evening by resting yesterday. You must refresh your mind with a journey to the Land of Nod. I will wake you at the appropriate hour."

Thus admonished, I retired to my old room and immediately collapsed onto the comfort of my bed of so many years, still in my evening clothes.

When I awoke later in the morning, I found a complete change of my own daily wear, hung on the back my dressing chair. Holmes had obviously sent 'round to my house for it whilst I slept.

After a quick toilet and change I strode into our sitting room to find a note from Holmes that read thusly:

> Watson,
>
> I am off to Bart's and then on to the Lyceum. Catch up
> when you can.
>
> S.H.

Just then, Mrs. Hudson poked her head in the doorway and spied me reading Holmes's missive.

"Good morning, Doctor," she said, "Mr. Holmes explained to me about your poor Mary. How is she?"

Declining breakfast and taking just the hot tea, which she had so instinctively prepared for me, I replied that Mary was much better and that I was about to be off to see her.

"Well, you give her my best and let me know if there is anything I can do. She can even stay here with me should need be."

"Mrs. Hudson, you are indeed a treasure and a saint." Then remembering my charge of the previous evening I added, "There may be a young lad coming by, by the name of Drew. I have instructed him to keep an eye out for anything suspicious at the theatre and report here. He's an eager boy and may be a bit impulsive, but I'm sure you will be able to set him at ease."

"Another 'Irregular' is he?" she answered smiling. "Not to worry, sir. I'll take good care of him and any message he might bring."

"I repeat, you are a saint." Handing her my empty teacup I retrieved Ferguson's coat and started off for the hospital.

* * *

At St. Bartholomew's I found Mary awake and alert, though weakened by her ordeal.

51

"John!" she cried, upon spying my head peeking through the door.

Quickly, I rushed to her bedside and held her in my arms, relieved at her improved condition. When we parted our words came out in a rush and we stumbled over each other's questions and answers until at last she enquired about Lilly.

"She was improving but still unconscious when I left this morning."

"Would you please check on her, John? I'm so worried after all she's been through."

"Of course, my Love, I'll be right back."

A few quick steps down the hall found me at Miss Fontaine's doorway where I noted Ferguson, dozing in an armchair and the actress still unconscious. I set Ferguson's coat on the foot of the bed and stepped back out into the hallway. Finding a nurse I enquired about our patient's condition and was told that she was improving and still receiving measured doses of a general antidote. Dr. Kennedy had taken over dayshift duties from Eckstein and was keeping an eye on her.

I thanked the nurse and strode back to Mary's room to give her my report. She was grateful, but still worried for her friend.

"John, is there nothing else to be done?" she implored.

"I'm afraid not at this time, my Love. Unless we discover the exact poison the general antidote will have to do. The good news is that she is responding so there's every chance of recovery."

We continued to chat awhile and as I was about to leave and let Mary rest Ferguson appeared. His tall frame took up much of the height of the doorway.

"Thank you, Doctor." He said, holding up his coat. Nodding to my wife he also stated, "Good to see you looking so much better, Ma'am."

Mary nodded in acknowledgement while I replied, "I thank you for the use of it. I see Miss Fontaine is improved somewhat."

"Yes, the doctors have full confidence in a complete recovery and have ordered me out of her room for a while, while they run some tests. I was thinking I should get back to the theatre to make sure everything is all right for tonight's performance. Can I drop you anywhere, Doctor?"

"As a matter of fact, I'm to meet Sherlock Holmes there. I shall be happy to accompany you, sir." After a kiss to my sweet Mary, we set off for the Lyceum.

While en route I queried Ferguson regarding his animosity toward Harrison Colby.

"It is an unfortunate fact that my parents once owned a furniture store next to one of Colby's theatres," responded the director. "A few years ago they suffered a fire and had to borrow against the mortgage to re-establish the business. It amounted to roughly one third of the value of the property. Somehow Colby acquired the note and has been hounding them ever since, because he wants to expand his theatre. They always make their payments on time, but he keeps sending lawyers after them with ridiculous demands. He's been trying to enlist my assistance by threatening to steal my actors or, in Lorraine's case, demanding her appearance due to the show she quit.

"My parents are gaining in age and cannot abide with his constant hounding. Certainly Loraine does not deserve such treatment for her courage in quitting his disgusting spectacle. The man is a snake and someday someone is going to crush him."

Chapter Six

Upon our arrival, we found the theatre abustle with various entertainers and stage crew. Irving had called for a morning rehearsal, with Lily Harley replacing the stricken Miss Fontaine. I had learned from Ferguson that the Sunday matinee was scheduled for variety acts only. The next play performance would not take place until that evening; therefore, he hoped to have the understudies well-versed in their roles by curtain time.

As Ferguson strode off to bring some semblance of order, I commenced my search for Holmes and found him engaged in conversation with an agitated Henry Irving and Inspector Lestrade of Scotland Yard.

Obviously, Holmes had run into one of Lestrade's stubborn streaks and implored me to supplement his accounting.

"Ah, Watson!" cried my friend, "At last. Please be good enough to bring the Inspector up to date on Miss Fontaine's condition and your verification that she was indeed poisoned, not the mere victim of 'the vapours' or some such female nonsense."

"I have just come from the hospital, Inspector," I stated, "where Miss Fontaine and my wife Mary are recovering from symptoms of poisoning. Mary is well on the road to recovery, but Miss Fontaine is still unconscious, though improving. Both Dr. Eckstein and I have confirmed the poison."

Lestrade seemed taken a bit aback at this confirmation of Holmes' claims and tried to recover by asking more questions.

"Indeed, Doctor? Well then … ahem, do you know what type of poison and how it was administered?"

"As I said, Lestrade," intoned Holmes, "the milk was certainly one agent of delivery."

"One agent, Mr. Holmes?" the Inspector smirked. "How many poisoners do you suppose we have in this theatre?"

"I'll reserve my answer to that, Lestrade, when I have all the facts. In the meantime, I suggest you pay heed to Mr. Irving's request and treat all the unfortunate incidents occurring to Miss Fontaine as criminal intentions and pursue your investigations."

"I'll do my job, Mr. Sherlock Holmes. And I'll brook no interference with official police business. Should you find anything of interest to this case, I'll thank you to report it to the Yard." Then Lestrade turned on his heel and marched off.

"Bloody fool!" mumbled the producer.

"Patience, Irving," responded Holmes, "Lestrade is a good man with a strong sense of justice. He just needs to open his mind a bit and be more observant as well."

"If you say so, Holmes," he replied. "If you have no further need of me I should be off to oversee rehearsal."

"Ferguson has returned with me," I voiced to the flustered proprietor, "I'm sure he is taking things in hand as we speak."

"Very well, I assume, Doctor, there's no possibility of Miss Fontaine returning to perform tonight?"

"No not for some days at least, sir," I replied. "Even once she regains consciousness, her body will need to recover from the ordeal before taking on the rigours of the stage."

"I see. Thank God we've got Lily prepared as understudy. I will take my leave of you, gentlemen. Holmes, you have free reign of the building. Let me know if you need anything." With that, the redoubtable Mr. Irving strode off toward the stage.

"I was glad, Watson," Holmes said as he turned to me, "that your wife is responding well to treatment. Though she was asleep when I called at the hospital this morning, Dr. Kennedy assured me she is quite well and should fully recover quickly."

"Thank you, Holmes. I appreciate your concern."

"I confess it is not only friendship, although I have a great appreciation for your wife's unique gifts and your feelings toward her. Beyond that, I am going to need you with your wits about you on this case, and thoughts of Mrs. Watson in a serious condition would be far too distracting for you to be of use to me."

I sighed at Holmes's lack of social skills, but gamely answered, "What need do you have of me, Holmes?"

"I have several avenues to track. If you would be good enough to trace the origin of the flowers and all the particulars about their arrival and delivery to Miss Fontaine on stage, I should like to see where that thread goes. In the meantime, I will tug on a few others and see what I can unravel. Will you remain at Baker Street until your wife is able to return home?"

"I have patients who need my attention." I replied. "But I shall certainly assist your investigation and report to you daily."

"That will do, Watson! I shall leave you to your pursuits, if you will meet me in time for Mrs. Hudson's excellent tea with your findings." Bidding me adieu, he strode off in the opposite direction to Irving and left the building.

Before aligning my thoughts along the pursuit of bouquets of flowers, I made it a point to retrieve my overcoat, topper and cane from the coat check room. As I passed through the lobby, I found young Drew sweeping the carpet and he deftly retrieved my items for me.

"'Ere you go, Dr. Watson," he said, as he placed them on the counter. "Good as new. Nothin' goes missin' from this room while I'm around."

"Thank you, Drew." I replied as I felt the welcome relief of my cane taking some weight off my wounded leg. The long night and cold journey to Baker Street had stirred up my old souvenir of the Afghan campaign. Much as I detested the need of it, as a man of less than forty years, my trusty stick was good for more than just fashion on this day.

Turning to the task Holmes had lain before me, I took advantage of my lone Irregular and began my quest.

"Tell me, Drew, do you know anything about the flowers that were delivered to Miss Fontaine these past three Saturdays?"

Chapter Seven

Drew informed me that, while he did not personally handle the flowers for Miss Fontaine, he did see one of the actors, Leo the singing comic, hand them to the stage manager, who delivered them during the curtain call.

I had Drew escort me backstage where he pointed out the latter, a Mr. Figgins. He was talking to three people at once and seemed quite busy, as the matinee was only two hours away and his schedule had been disrupted by the extra rehearsal for the play's understudies.

Deciding to try my luck with him later, I asked Drew where I could find Leo the comic.

"He don't have any dressin' room to hisself, Doctor," the lad told me. "He's got a table space with the others, upstairs. He ain't likely to be in yet though. He generally shows up 'bout an hour before the variety performance."

"He has no part in the play then?" I asked.

"Oh, no sir! He's strictly a solo act. Sings funny songs and what not. He's been doin' a bit 'bout a Canadian Indian lately. "

"Very well, I'll wait for Mr. Figgins then. You can go on about your duties, Drew. Thank you."

As my eager colleague hopped off to work I strode over near Figgins and waited for an opportunity to get a word in. After nearly ten minutes, he at last seemed to have a brief respite and I introduced myself.

"Mr. Figgins, I'm Dr. John Watson. Could I have a moment?"

Figgins was a small man, perhaps five foot eight inches tall, with a wiry build, dark hair going grey at the temples. His long salt and pepper sideburns grew down into a completely grey moustache and prompted me to put his age near fifty. He was in shirtsleeves and braces with a bowler on his head and the short stub of a pipe in his mouth.

He gave me a once over look, noting my hat and cane, and queried, "Doctor, eh? What's your act? Magic? Hypnotism?"

Patiently I replied, "No, sir. I am Dr. **Watson**. I'm helping Sherlock Holmes on the Loraine Fontaine case."

He pointed at me with his pipe and said, "Oh yes. Mr. Irving told us about that. Sorry business that is. What can I do for you, Doctor?"

"I understand that you were the one who handed the flowers to Miss Fontaine these past three Saturdays at her curtain call."

"Yes, that was me. What about it?"

"Miss Fontaine told us there was never any card attached. Did you happen to notice any such card that may have fallen off? Or perhaps you know who they came from?"

He puffed on his pipe thoughtfully, "No," he said slowly, "There wasn't any card when I got them. Usually there would be, from some admiring bloke. But those particular bouquets were brought to me by Leo Dryden, the singer. I'm sure he just brought them up from whoever dropped them off. Not likely he would be giving them to Loraine himself."

"You're sure about that?" I asked, pondering a brief thought of a possible suspect.

"Well, I've no proof, if that's what you mean. But I believe the young man is much more interested in Lily Harley than our leading lady."

"Interesting." I replied, pulling out a notebook and jotting that bit of information down for future reference. "Thank you, sir. I shall let you return to your duties."

"That's it?" he asked with a puzzling frown. "You just wanted to know about some silly flowers?"

"For now, Mr. Figgins. It's an unanswered question and Mr. Holmes thrives on such things. I may get back to you at some other time. Do you know when we might expect Mr. Dryden to arrive?"

"Well matinee's at 2:00 so he isn't expected until 1:00. Although, if he heard about Lily getting bumped up to leading lady status he might be here any minute."

"Thank you. I'll just get out of your way now." I said, as Miss Harley came rushing up to Figgins with exasperation on her face.

"Why can't I move my things into the star dressing room, Mr. Figgins?" she demanded. "It's my right you know, until her *ladyship* returns."

Her tone was such that I stood discreetly within earshot to see where this little diatribe might lead. Figgins returned her glare eye to eye and replied. "First of all *Missy*, Miss Fontaine is still the star of this show until Mr. Irving tells me otherwise. Second of all, Scotland bloody Yard has sealed the room for its investigation, and third, if you expect to get on in the theatrical profession, you had best watch that tongue of yours. I've been in this business over thirty years and I've seen 'em come and I've seen 'em go, and your 'talent' isn't yet sufficient to be making bloody demands about star dressing rooms!" He then strode away, leaving the actress standing and fuming.

I should state that Miss Harley was about twenty-five years old and normally an attractive brunette with a notable singing voice. But at that particular moment her beauty was marred by her attitude and the look of near madness on her face. I recalled Holmes's comment of the night before and noted that this was looking more than a little suspicious. As I contemplated what I might do to follow this new thread, as Holmes would put it, Lionel Ferguson's voice boomed out from the stage, demanding Miss Harley's return.

Thus delayed from any pursuit of the Harley matter, I retrieved my watch from my waistcoat pocket and noted that it was just past noon. This was not the timepiece I had once described in my early writings – the one that Holmes had made so many deductions from, regarding its passage through the lives of my father and brother. This was a fine gold watch that had been a wedding present from my sweet Mary, and I sighed and said a quick prayer as I closed its case.

Since there was no sign of the comedian, I felt this was the perfect opportunity to seek some quick repast, having not indulged in my usual hearty breakfast. I left the theatre and returned home to deposit my evening coat and hat and then proceeded to a nearby restaurant, where I commenced to devour a fine halibut steak, boiled potato and a variety of vegetables.

* * *

I returned to the theatre at about twenty past one and immediately began to seek out the singing comedian, Dryden. I soon found the man sitting before a mirror, a can of makeup in his right hand. His face was covered in reddish-orange greasepaint, and he was darkening his eyebrows to make them more visible to the audience. Yet something about him seemed familiar.

"Excuse me, Mr. Dryden?" I enquired, making myself heard above the hubbub of the crowded dressing area where it seemed all the acts shared space.

"Yes?" he answered, continuing his perusal in the mirror as he applied the charcoal-like substance to his otherwise brown hair.

"My name," I replied, dodging a unicyclist weaving his way through the crowd, "is Dr. John Watson. I understand you have been delivering flowers for Miss Fontaine these past few weeks."

I looked carefully at the mirror to see his reaction to that statement, which I had obviously delivered as a half-truth to see what it might uncover.

He stopped, dropping his hands to the tabletop, and focused on me via my reflection in the mirror with a quizzical look on his face. He then busied himself with the application of what appeared to be Indian war paint.

"That's not quite accurate, Doctor," he stated. "I picked up flowers that were delivered at the stage door and brought them to Figgins for delivery to Miss Fontaine at her curtain call. She gets them quite often you know. Most leading ladies do."

He then turned and looked directly at me asking, "And what business of it is yours, if I may ask?"

"I am helping to treat Miss Fontaine and she has been curious as to whom these rose and lily arrangements have been coming from. Mr. Figgins tells me there has been no card. How did you know they were for Miss Fontaine?"

He hesitated just a bit and turned back to the mirror, checking his makeup again, "The delivery boy said they were for her. He didn't leave a name and I didn't notice if there was a card or not. I just took them to old Figgy."

"It strikes me as curious, that you should manage to be about the back entrance every Saturday night when the flower delivery happens to arrive."

"Nothing curious about it, Doctor. By that time the play is over and I hang around the back door waiting for… that is, to see if there are any of my fellow thespians who might be going out to eat, so I might join in the party. If a delivery boy comes, it's no skin off my nose to accept his package and pass it on to the rightful person."

The obvious question in my mind at that point would have been to ask if he was waiting for Lily Harley, but with the crowded room it seemed this was not the ideal time, nor place, to press that point. I felt it could wait until I could catch the man alone or perhaps Holmes would wish to pursue a different tack.

Thus I merely stated, "So it was the delivery boy who told you the flowers were for Miss Fontaine and there was no card?"

"As I said, Doctor," he replied, standing and beginning to move toward the door, "I didn't notice a card. The boy said they were for Fontaine and I just gave them to Figgy. Now, if you'll excuse me, I have a show to prepare for." He then turned on his heel and left the room.

63

It seemed curious to me that such an unusual bouquet would arrive without some identification of the sender. I decided to keep backtracking along this trail and descended the stairs from the general dressing area to make my way to the back door.

The guardian of the stage door was a large fellow named Washburn, near on to six and one half feet in height and weighing close to eighteen stone. I introduced myself and told him I was seeking the origin of the flowers that had been coming recently for Miss Fontaine.

"There's lots of flowers coming in for the lady, and some others too. How's she feeling by the way? She's a nice lady that one. Not so stuck up like some of them others."

I told him that she was recovering, but would not be back to work for awhile.

"I'm particularly looking for whoever sent the roses with the single lily these past three Saturdays. Miss Fontaine is very curious and would like to thank the person if she only knew who it was. I believe Mr. Dryden took the delivery?"

"Oh yeah, Leo was here. He's a nice enough chap. Took them flowers out to Old Figgy, so's I could stay at me post. That's when it gets a bit dicey you know, people trying to get in to see the actors and such after the play. Or hangin' about outside the door and pestering folks for autographs."

"So did you see if there was a card with the roses? There wasn't any when Miss Fontaine received them."

"Well, most times there's a card with flowers when they show up. But I didn't notice in particular. Leo took 'em from the boy and then off to the stage."

"Did you recognize the delivery boy? Do you know what shop he was from?"

The big man stood and gave an eye to a couple members of the stage crew who had just come in the door.

"'Scuse me, Doctor. Just makin' sure no one's trying to sneak by," he said as he lowered his great bulk with a creak back onto his stool, "All them boys look pretty much the same, unless some fancy lord or someone sends about one of his servants. Did you talk to Leo?"

"Yes, I've just met with Mr. Dryden. He wasn't particularly helpful."

"Really? That's an odd bit."

"Why's that, sir?"

"Well, Leo's usually a good bloke. Always hangin' about and doin' a lot more than most actors to help out the stage crew and such. I'm surprised he wouldn't be more helpful seein' it was him that drove Miss Fontaine to hospital last night.

Chapter Eight

That revelation from Washburn took me aback and then I realized why Dryden had seemed familiar. The vermillion face makeup had hidden his features from me and I had paid no particular attention to our driver the night before except when he had turned into the wrong street. Even then, he was wearing a grey overcoat with a black flat cap pulled down on his forehead and a tartan scarf about his chin. So all I really had to go by was the man's voice, muffled as it was by the scarf.

Thus armed with all this information, I took my leave of Washburn and decided to question the flower shops between the theatre and St. Bartholomew's where I intended to check on Mary and Miss Fontaine and then report back to Baker Street for my rendezvous with Holmes.

The two florist's shops I encountered en route to St. Bartholomew's proved fruitless in the placement of any orders for a lily and rose combination. Arriving at the hospital I immediately rushed to Mary's room only to find it empty with the bed freshly made.

Somewhat shaken by this sight, I retreated again to the hallway to seek out a nurse. As I passed Miss Fontaine's open door, I glanced in that direction and spied an orderly. Entering the room, I began to ask about Mary when I saw her sitting next to the actress' bed, holding her hand. She looked up and smiled at me. I cannot tell you the immensity of the relief that lightened my heart.

"John darling," she said quietly and a little hoarsely, "Lilly is much better. She woke up around noon. The doctors say her symptoms have greatly improved, but there remains a weakness they cannot explain. They've given her some sleeping medication for now."

"Mary my Love, what are you doing here? You should be in bed yourself!" I said as I held her in my arms.

"Yes, *Doctor*," she said, smiling, straightening my tie and kissing my cheek. "I soon will be. The orderly is making up the other bed in this room so I can stay by Lilly's side."

"But you shouldn't be out of bed at all!" I protested.

"Nonsense, John, I'm fine, just feeling a little weak and my throat is very sore. Dr. Kennedy says I should able to leave in day or so. In the meantime, I can keep Lilly company and," she added, lowering her voice conspiratorially, "I can keep an eye on her visitors for you and Mr. Holmes."

"She's had visitors?" I replied. "Who?"

"See, I knew you would want to know." She winked at me. "So far only her maidservant, Caroline. She brought her father's watch and made sure it was wound and ticking when she placed it there on the table."

I gazed to where she indicated and the watch was ticking away, rather loudly for it was old, just an arm's length away from Miss Fontaine's sleeping form.

I pulled Mary farther away from the orderly's ears and whispered, "But it could be dangerous, Mary! You know someone is out to harm her!"

"Exactly, John, and unless you or Mr. Holmes or Scotland Yard intend to post a guard here, who better to keep an eye out than I? There's a nurse's call bell next to my bed and I can summon help in an instant. As a patient myself, no one would suspect that I was keeping watch."

"No!" I exclaimed "It's too dangerous. I'll stay here myself."

"John Hamish Watson, you listen to me. This is something *I* can do. Mr. Holmes needs you to help him catch the person who did this. That's the only way to keep her truly safe." When my better half gets a certain tilt of her head, a determined look upon her face and uses my full name, I know that further debate is useless. Therefore I grudgingly acquiesced to her perseverance.

I helped her into the freshly made up bed, which was separated from her sleeping friend by about six feet. She was feeling the effects of moving about so soon after her own treatment so we talked only briefly. I mentioned there was poison in the milk and it reacted with her tea to cause her symptoms, but we were still at a loss to explain why Miss Fontaine had such a strong and opposite reaction. I said Holmes was looking into the rose thorns but had not shared any conclusion with me as yet.

"You should go to your meeting with him, John." She said. "I'll be fine. I just need some rest. Go on. It will take you a while at this time of day."

I leaned over and kissed her lips gently. "I love you."

"And I love you, my husband," she said, placing her hand on my cheek and looking deep into my eyes. "Be careful."

"You, too," I replied and surreptitiously blew her another kiss as I stepped out into the corridor.

*   *   *

Arriving at Baker Street at quarter to four, I purchased the afternoon edition of the Times from a nearby newsboy and went upstairs to await Holmes's arrival. At precisely four o'clock, Mrs. Hudson arrived with a tray full of all the proper ingredients for a Sunday afternoon tea. Just as she was leaving, the world's finest consulting detective strode into the room and plopped into the chair opposite me.

"Ah, Watson, dear fellow, you are certainly a far cheerier soul than when you arrived at this morning's ungodly hour. Obviously, your wife is doing better after receiving your afternoon visit. How is Miss Fontaine faring?"

69

I replied that Miss Fontaine was somewhat improved, having come out of her coma-like state and then asked, "How did you know that I'd been to the hospital again this afternoon and not just this morning?"

"Please, old friend, it's elementary. The fact that you have come from the hospital within the hour is quite evident from the antiseptic smell that clings to your clothing like a familiar overcoat, and your countenance is much lighter which is easily explained by the improvement of your wife's condition. Now, pray tell, what news have you for me?"

As I told him of my encounters at the theatre, he seemed to take a great interest in the characters of Miss Harley and Mr. Dryden.

"Those threads may be more interwoven than a first glance reveals, Watson. I believe I shall attend the play again this evening. This time however, from backstage."

"Is there anything I can do, Holmes?"

"I was hoping your investigation of the flowers would have been more fruitful. But then, if the thorns truly were poisoned, the sender would have insured the delivery method to be untraceable.

"However, Watson, I have another thread to pull that will require a trip to St. Albans on the morrow. My investigations into our poison plant have been nearly exhausted as far as London is concerned. Therefore, my friend, I do have a task for you."

He reached into his pocket and tore some pages off his notepad and handed them to me.

"I obtained this data from Miss Fontaine's apartment with the help of young Caroline," he said. "Since you will undoubtedly be spending much of the day at Bart's, I trust you can give your wife an hour or two's respite and step over a few streets to the Records Office. Find out what you can about these properties. Current occupants, rental income, land value, that sort of thing. Then please drop in on this gentleman." He added, handing me a card, "

"T. James Salmon, Solicitor," I read aloud. "Who is he Holmes?"

"Mr. Salmon is Miss Fontaine's, or to use her legal name, Miss Fields' lawyer. See if you can ascertain any issues she's having with any of her tenants, or even the rascal Harrison Colby whom she mentioned. You should also determine if she has drawn up a will and who the beneficiaries might be."

"In other words, I'm on a hunt for motive."

"Excellent, Watson." said Holmes sipping his tea. "Tonight I shall ascertain what I can of theatrical threats and tomorrow night we shall meet again to compare notes. Let us say, seven o'clock at Simpson's for dinner?"

"That sounds delightful, Holmes!" I replied, then asked "What will you be doing in St. Albans?"

"Looking for the root cause of our thorny problem." He smiled, and lit his pipe with that expression that said I would get no more than that out of him on this evening.

Chapter Nine

While I returned to St. Bartholomew's that evening for a last visit with Mary and to renew my discussions with Eckstein, Holmes was off to the Lyceum to pursue further investigations.

Arriving at the theatre an hour before the play was slated to begin, Holmes first action was to return to the dressing room of Miss Fontaine. As he approached, the door suddenly opened from within and out stepped the lively Inspector Lestrade.

"Ah, Mr. Holmes!" the Inspector intoned in his high pitched voice. "I've been over the room with a fine toothed comb and was about to release it back to Mr. Irving's use. I assume you are quite finished as well?"

"Yes, Lestrade," Holmes answered. "I believe I gleaned all I could last night. Did you draw any conclusions from your search?"

"I did note that the gas pipe was marred severely near the joint. No true pipefitter would let his spanner slip like that. Seems to me an obvious sign of tampering."

"Yes," said Holmes, "I agree. Did you also note that our sloppy gas man used his left-hand to loosen the pipes?"

"Eh, no, Mr. Holmes. How did you come by that conclusion?" said Lestrade somewhat contritely.

"Observe the marks made by the slipping spanner, Inspector," Holmes replied, pointing his cane through the open door at the overhead line near the joint. "Note the direction of the scratches. Only a man using his left-hand would have left such marks in that direction."

"Left-handed? Hmm. Well, be that as it may I must admit that on top of the poisoning confirmed by the doctor, it appears to be a criminal act."

"Will you be posting a guard at Miss Fontaine's hospital room, then?" enquired Holmes.

"That's just what I was about to do," replied the somewhat chagrined Inspector. "Mr. Holmes, I cannot deny that you've been a bit of a help to the force in the past and I would like to apologize for my tone last evening. This Bow Street Police Strike on top of the move to New Scotland Yard has us all a bit on edge."

"I quite understand, Inspector. But about that guard ..."

Just then a female voice pierced the air as it approached the two detectives.

"Ah, there you are! Have you finished playing with Loraine's things yet? When will that dressing room be free to use?"

Lestrade looked the spritely figure up and down and replied "And just what business would that be of yours, Miss? Who are you anyway?"

Before she could answer Holmes stepped in, doffing his hat, and said in his most gracious tone, "Inspector Lestrade of Scotland Yard, allow me to introduce Miss Lily Harley. Miss Harley is Loraine Fontaine's understudy and will thus be taking over her role until the lady returns. I believe that the 'law of the theatre' would therefore deed that dressing room to her for the time being."

Miss Harley, disarmed by Holmes manner, remarked more civilly, "The gentleman is quite right. Thank you, sir. Whom do I have the pleasure of addressing?"

"Sherlock Holmes, at your service madam."

Lestrade piped up at this point. "Well, I'm quite done here and I don't know about the 'law of the theatre', but I'll be letting Mr. Irving know that the room is quite usable. You'll have to take it up with him."

The Inspector turned to go but Holmes laid a hand on his arm, "A moment if you please, Lestrade. Excuse me, Miss Harley, I would like to continue our conversation but I need to convey something to the Inspector."

The two men drew off to the side for a minute as Miss Harley stepped into the dressing room. When Holmes and Lestrade parted company, my friend returned to Miss Harley's presence.

"So, Miss Harley," remarked Holmes, "are you ready for your debut as the leading lady?"

The young brunette sat in the dressing chair and looked at herself in the mirror.

"I fully intend to be, Mr. Holmes. My career was put on hold last year while I gave birth to my second son. I've got to make good for his and his brother's sake."

"Your husband is hard pressed to make ends meet?" enquired the Detective.

She looked up at his tall figure and smiled shyly as she bowed her head and returned her gaze to the mirror. "Kind of you to assume I was married, Mr. Holmes." She stated as she rubbed an empty ring finger. "We've been separated for a bit now. He's performing down in Liverpool and I've not heard from him in four months."

"The mark of your wedding ring is still upon your finger, Miss Harley. So much so, that I can only presume you still wear it and only take it off for the sake of your character's performance."

She looked at him in the mirror. "You are a very observant man, Mr. Holmes. That's the exact truth of it. Are you a policeman?"

Holmes lowered his eyes and let a fleeting smile pass over his lips and shook his head. "No, madam, I'm merely an observer. Tell me, do you have any apprehension about taking this part, or for that matter, using this dressing room?"

"Apprehension?" she said, lifting an eyebrow, "Why no, Mr. Holmes. I would have done anything for this role but Ferguson's so smitten with Loraine that I was dropped to her understudy after the auditions. I may be a bit nervous to do well, but that's normal for any actress."

"I'm sure," he replied, "But I was referring to the deliberate attempts on Miss Fontaine's life."

"What *are* you talking about?" she asked quizzically.

"The leaking gas for one and the fact that she was poisoned last night."

The look on Miss Harley's face was one of dismay. "Poisoned? But I thought she just took sick. She hasn't been well for some time you know."

"I'm afraid poison has been confirmed, Madam. A chance break for you, but you should take care. Incidentally," Holmes said quietly, as he turned to leave, "who is *your* understudy?"

* * *

At the hospital that evening, I found my Mary in excellent spirits and Miss Fontaine awake, but obviously weakened by her condition. The two of them were speaking quietly when I arrived.

"John, dear!" my wife exclaimed, "See how much better Lilly is. We've been catching up on the last few years."

I hugged her and turned to Miss Fontaine, "It's good to see you awake, Miss Fontaine. You gave us a bit of a scare. How are you feeling?"

"I'm a bit nauseous and feel weak, Doctor, but Mary's company has been a godsend. I'm sure I'll recover soon."

"As am I, Miss Fontaine." came a voice from the doorway. Dr. Eckstein strolled into the room, papers in hand. "Good to see you again, Watson. I can tell you that your wife is recovering very nicely and should be able to go home tomorrow or Tuesday at the latest."

"That's excellent news." I cried, beaming and taking my wife's hand.

She squeezed my palm and replied, "I should like to keep Lilly company if you can spare the bed, Doctor."

Eckstein looked at me puzzled and I quickly explained Mary's plan to be a watchful guardian over any visitors while Miss Fontaine was confined to bed. He pondered for a moment and finally said, "I suppose we can manage that, although I assure you the hospital staff are quite capable."

"Capable they may be, Doctor," she stated matter-of-factly. "But they are also busy with duties to their other patients. I can devote myself entirely to Lillian's care."

"Very well. Now as to your condition, Miss Fontaine," he said, turning to face the actress, "we've managed to isolate your symptoms to specific types of poisonous chemicals."

Miss Fontaine clutched her throat at the thought and nodded for the doctor to go on.

"The milk that Mr. Holmes sent us showed traces of one type of poison that, in small doses, would have eventually incapacitated you and possibly lead to your death."

"That's monstrous!" cried Mary. "How could anyone do such a thing?"

I attempted to calm my wife and reassure Miss Fontaine. "That is what Holmes is seeking to discover at this very moment, my Love. Rest assured, Miss Fontaine, Sherlock Holmes will not rest while your life is in danger."

Eckstein continued his revelations. "I believe that your weakened condition from your exposure to the gas leak, and infection by a second chemical, caused your lapse into unconsciousness. Watson, the books you left open gave me a clue that could explain why Miss Fontaine's symptoms were so opposite to your wife's. Although the blood tests were inconclusive, I believe that this second chemical was introduced into Miss Fontaine's bloodstream through the puncture wound from the rose thorn."

"She was poisoned *twice*?" I responded, "That's hard to believe."

"Even so," he replied, "I believe that second exposure actually saved her life. Had it not reacted to her already infected body and caused the coma, the original poisoning might never have been discovered. It would have continued to build up until it was too late."

"Oh, my God!" Miss Fontaine cried collapsing onto her back in the bed.

Immediately, Mary rushed from her own bed and held her friend's hand, trying to calm her down.

Eckstein pulled a packet from his pocket, poured it into a glass of water and held it to his patient's lips. She drank it grudgingly and wiped her mouth with her sleeve.

"What *was* that?" she implored with a disgusted look upon her face.

"Just something to calm your nerves," he answered. "It will probably make you sleepy, so you should try to relax and get a good night's rest. I know this has been a trying ordeal for you, but I thought it best to tell you while you had friends here to help. It will take some time, but you should make a full recovery and be back on stage soon."

"If some madman doesn't kill me first!" she wept.

Mary put her arm around her friend's shoulders and held her closely. "There, there, Lilly, we won't let anything like that happen. You said it yourself. Mr. Holmes is a godsend. I'm sure he'll catch whoever is doing this soon," she reasoned, looking at me for confirmation.

"Indeed, Miss Fontaine, Holmes is at the theatre this very moment on your case. In fact," I pulled one of my cards from my pocket and handed it to her with a pencil, "Holmes has entrusted me to visit your solicitor tomorrow to look for possible reasons why anyone would wish you harm. If you could just jot a note to him on the back of my card giving your permission for me to do so, I'm sure that will allow me to pursue that avenue so much easier."

By thus distracting her from the thoughts racing through her mind she calmed somewhat and wrote out her consent. I returned the card and pencil to my waistcoat pocket with a 'Thank you' and assured her that all would be well.

"John, I'm going to walk Lilly to the ladies' room, please wait for me."

"Certainly, my Love, I'll just be out in the hall with Dr. Eckstein."

She slowly helped her friend out of bed while Eckstein and I retreated to the hallway.

Once out of earshot from the ladies, Eckstein confided to me. "Thank you for your help there, Watson. I hadn't planned on telling her just yet, but with the two of you there to support her, I felt it was an opportune moment."

"Of course," I replied. "Although I have a feeling that Mary may not have agreed with your timing."

He nodded, "Oftentimes the women do know best. But, I felt she needed to be aware of the risk to her should she try to do something foolish like go back to work. I know how stubborn actors can be. 'The show must go on', and all that."

"Yes, I myself have treated such people who insisted that they had to go on stage in spite of broken bones, high fevers and other assorted ailments. Performers are certainly a different breed."

"They are indeed, Watson." Turning more directly to face me, he lowered his voice. "There is something else I wished to discuss with you as well. Are you sure your wife has not exhibited any signs of weakness or fainting spells prior to this incident?"

Startled by his question I could only stammer "No, not that I … wait, there was an incident two years ago, the night we first met, but she had been through a series of shocking experiences on that evening and her reaction seemed quite natural. Why, is something wrong?"

"Her heart murmur seems a bit strong for someone of her age. I'm only concerned that, if this is a new symptom, rather than something she's been living with, it could indicate the beginning of a more serious problem."

My mind would not accept the implications of his statement and I could only answer with false bravado, "Her father had a heart condition. Perhaps it is hereditary."

"Ah, that could very likely be the case. In any event, I was going to suggest keeping her here to make sure the poison hasn't triggered some adverse effect upon her system. Her concern for her friend will make that convenient, without causing her any undue stress, until we're sure."

79

"Shouldn't we tell her so that she can report any further symptoms?" I proposed.

"Bed rest should be best for her right now. Her worry of Miss Fontaine is quite enough. I'd rather not add to that without proof that there is a legitimate problem."

I agreed with my colleague, and as he turned to go to attend to other patients he stated, "Be assured I will keep you apprised, Doctor. Please let me know how Mr. Holmes investigation turns out."

He strode off and I returned to the room to await the ladies. Soon Mary was helping her former roommate back into bed and turning down the lights by half. I helped Mary back into her own bed and we spoke briefly.

"Tell me, John, what progress has Mr. Holmes made?" she whispered quietly as the drugs were sending her friend off to a peaceful slumber.

"Holmes is on some track which is taking him off to St. Albans tomorrow." I answered, "He implied that it has something to do with the poisoned flowers. I'll be going to the Records Office to check on properties that she owns. After that, I will meet her solicitor to ascertain who might benefit from her demise."

"Does he think the motive may be money, then? I had no idea that she was that well off."

"I don't believe he has narrowed down a motive yet. He was also going to be questioning people at the theatre tonight. Especially her understudy."

"Oh, John, I can't believe someone would kill for a part in a play."

"As I was just discussing with Eckstein, my dear, actors are a different breed."

Chapter Ten

Later that evening, shortly after ten o'clock, Mary, who spent the time reading while her friend slept under the influence of Eckstein's drug, drifted off herself. But within the hour she awoke, sensing a presence in the room which she presumed to be the nurse, as the light she had been reading by was lowered to a mere glow. When she opened her eyes however, the figure bending over Miss Fontaine was not the feminine form she expected, but a large man dressed in black who was neither, Doctors Eckstein or Kennedy.

With his back to her she slipped her covers off slowly without a sound and watched, ready to spring to action if this intruder intended any harm. She confessed to me later that, with no weapon at hand, her plan was to reach for the brass nurses' bell on the table with one hand while bringing her heavy book down on the assailant's head with the other, hoping to catch him off guard long enough for help to arrive.

The invader of their hospital room then bent his barrel-chested torso farther over the prone figure of Miss Fontaine. Silently he curled his fingers around the sheets and blankets, pulling them slowly toward the actress's head.

As his body turned in this motion Mary let out a gasp of recognition. The dark imposing figure settled the blanket around Miss Fontaine's neck and turned toward Mary holding a finger to his lips.

What Mary had glimpsed in periphery was now full toward her in recognition as a Police Constable's uniform, its bright silver buttons aglow in the soft light. The round face that beamed in a noticeable grin was that of Frederick MacDonald, who motioned Mary to follow him out to the hallway where he retrieved his helmet and baton from a waiting bench. He then bade my bride to sit down.

As soon as she did so her voice found itself and in a rush she blurted, "Mr. MacDonald you gave me a fright. I was about to leap to Lilly's defence before I recognized your uniform. How did you come to be here?"

In his thick Scotsman's burr he replied, "Ah Mrs. Watson, 'twas Inspector Lestrade himself who asked me to keep on eye on you and the lass. Though I suspect it was at Mr. Holmes's request."

"I'm sure it was," she answered. "Will you be on guard all night then?"

"Aye, mum, though not always in sight, but surely within earshot. So you just ring that bell or cry out and I'll be at your side afore ye can say 'William Wallace was a wily warrior'."

"Thank you, Mr. Mac, I'll sleep much sounder knowing you're on duty. Thank you also, for tucking Lilly in. I'll be off to bed then."

"Pardon me, mum, I thought the lass's name was Loraine?"

Taking the policeman's proffered hand she stood and said "Her stage name is Loraine Fontaine, but her real name is Lillian Fields, though I suppose very few people would know that except someone from her past."

"Lilly Fields," he grinned. "I like it. She never should have changed a fine name like that. A natural beauty of a name it is. Ah well, that's actresses for ye. Good night, Mrs. Watson. Sleep well and have no fear."

"That I shall. Thank you, kind sir."

Of course this little adventure of Mary's was related to me at a later time. The morning after it took place found me at the Public Record Office in Chancery Lane. Here I found two properties listing Lillian Fields. One of these was a cotton farm near Huntingdon, where she was shown to be landlord. The other a resort, noted for its mineral springs, down in the Epsom area, where she was listed as a partial owner.

I then ventured to the offices of Anderson, Erstad and Salmon to look into Miss Fontaine's financial and legal affairs. Upon my arrival, I stepped into a well-appointed waiting room. Directly in front of me was a raised platform where a young gentleman was seated at a desk surrounded by fine oak panelling. It gave the appearance of a magistrate's bench and was elevated enough to keep prying eyes from perusing the clerk's work. He rose, stretching his tall, thin frame and smoothing his suit, stepped down to the floor level and introduced himself.

"Good afternoon, sir. I am Mr. Shields. May I be of assistance?

"Good afternoon." I said "My name is Dr. John Watson. I'm here on behalf of Miss Lillian Fields and was wondering if I could speak with Mr. Salmon."

"Do you have an appointment?" he asked.

"No, this matter came up rather quickly over the weekend and I had hoped to obtain a few minutes with him."

"Let me call his assistant for you and see what can be arranged." At which point, he returned to his desk and rang a bell three times.

Immediately from off to my right, an eager young lad in his early twenties came through an archway and reported to Shields like a recruit to his sergeant.

"Wooten," said Shields, "this is Dr. Watson. He would like to arrange to see Mr. Salmon. Would you please take care of him?"

"Yes, Mr. Shields. This way, Doctor." He bowed slightly and indicated I should follow him to the adjoining foyer.

"Begging your pardon sir," said the apprentice as he led me to his desk "but would you be the Dr. John Watson whose story was in *Lippincott's* magazine?"

Modestly I replied, "Why yes, Mr. Wooten. Did you enjoy it?"

"Oh, it was fascinating. But it seemed a bit fantastic. Certainly no one could be as clever and observant as you make your character of Holmes to be. But I certainly enjoyed it."

Startled by his statement as he showed me to a chair while he sat behind his desk, I dropped my gloves into my hat and set it on the table next to me. "Do I conclude that you believe Mr. Holmes to be a fictional character, sir?"

"Why, certainly," he said hesitantly.

Crossing my legs and assuming what I confess to be a fair imitation of a pose that Holmes takes when in a lecturing mode, I answered. "Sherlock Holmes is as real as you and I. My whole purpose for being here today is to assist him on his most recent case."

Embarrassed he stammered, "Uh, very well, Doctor. Mr. Salmon has been out all morning and I do not expect him back for a bit. What business did you wish to discuss? Perhaps I can help."

I retrieved the card from my pocket where Miss Fields had given her permission and handed it across to him. "Mr. Holmes's client, probably best known to you as the actress, Lorraine Fontaine, has given her permission for us to look into the state of her affairs, in connection with an attempt on her life. She is currently in hospital and has thus given me this note as my *bona fides*."

Wooten took the note nervously. "Someone tried to kill Miss Fontaine? Is she all right?"

"She is well for now. We are looking into the case on her behalf."

"Thank goodness," he replied, examining the note "Yes, this is Miss Fontaine's signature. I have a picture of hers which she graciously signed when she was here in the office one time. I'll get her file and we'll see if there's anything there that will help you."

As he left me sitting while he retrieved our client's records I let my gaze wander about the room. The thought occurred to me to see if I could practice a bit of Holmes' observation techniques. I studied the room with more thoroughness than usual. The solid hardwood floor was well varnished with a bit of wear showing at the doorway. The rugs were of good quality and appeared to be Persian. There were heavy bookshelves containing both legal volumes and occasional knick knacks; small statuettes, busts, and other ornamental pieces, primarily of historical figures of the British Empire. On the wall behind Wooten's desk was a framed document declaring that Mr. Shawn Wooten was a recent graduate of Cambridge. The door in that wall was open to Mr. Salmon's office, where I spied an ornate oak desk with shelves of law books behind. Something about the room though, seemed odd. On the pretence of stretching my legs I rose and wandered a bit to my left where I had a better view inside. Was it an optical illusion or was the desk slanted forward? As my gaze dropped to the feet of the desk I realized that, while the front legs were intact, extending some six inches below the front panel, the legs on occupant's side were only an inch below where I would presume bottom drawers would open.

As I pondered the meaning of this, young Wooten returned with an envelope containing the firm's records for Miss Lillian Fields. We pored over the documents therein which among others, reiterated the ownership she held in certain properties. I was at a loss as to what, if any meaning these documents might have for my celebrated colleague, when I remembered I was looking for motive. The only motive apparent was the ownership of the property she held.

I asked the young clerk, "What happens to these properties in the event of Miss Fields' demise?"

He picked through some papers and pulled one out. "There is a note here from Mr. Salmon that he advised Miss Fields to draw up a will last year, but there is no will on file as yet. In the absence of such a document I believe her father's will orders the property back to her mother's care or to be split amongst some cousins should her mother not be alive at the time of Miss Fields' passing."

This certainly shed some light on our case. I wrote this information down to relay to Holmes. As I stood to leave I thanked Mr. Wooten and thought to take a stab in the dark regarding his employer.

"I noticed Mr. Salmon has an unusual desk. Might I take a closer look?"

Wooten grinned as if at some secret and showed me to the office door. "Mr. Salmon never leaves anything out on his desk so you may examine it if you wish. But please do not open any of the drawers."

While he watched, I strode over to the desk, nearly stumbling as I drew near. I then realized that there was a slight incline in the floor. This explained the shorter legs at the back of the desk in order to keep it level. Examination of the chair proved revealing as well. Looking down at the carpet, I viewed the pattern of wear. I then looked at the placement of the volumes on the shelf behind the chair. Proceeding around the room I was examining a painting when Wooten spoke up.

"What would Mr. Holmes have to say about your findings, Doctor?"

Keeping my back to him I stated, "Mr. Salmon is a middle-aged man who has recently had his hair cut. He is right-handed, walks with a slight limp and is approximately five foot two inches tall."

I turned to face my questioner and found the five foot two inch tall T. James Salmon standing next to him with a glower on his face.

"What goes on here? Who are you sir?"

Wooten spoke up and said, "This is Dr. John Watson, sir. He is working for Miss Lillian Fields and came by to check some records, with Miss Field's permission."

"I see," replied Salmon somewhat mollified, "but what is this act of charlatanism, that you pretend to deduce such facts without having met me. Surely you must have seen me at some time to know these things."

Stepping over to the doorway I gave him a slight bow and said "I assure you sir, that I was merely applying Sherlock Holmes' methods of observation and deduction as a demonstration to the young man. I have never laid eyes on you before this moment."

"Who the devil is Sherlock Holmes?"

Again Wooten spoke up "Mr. Sherlock Holmes is a private detective sir. Dr. Watson wrote about him in *Lippincott's* magazine a few months ago."

"*Lippincott's* is well known for its fiction, Wooten." He stated brusquely, as he removed his coat and strode up the incline to sit behind his desk.

Looking to me again he stated "A 'private' detective you say? I thought such things were the responsibility of Scotland Yard. You say you were hired by Lillian Fields?"

"Yes, Mr. Salmon," I answered "There has been an attempt, possibly more than one, on her life. She is currently in hospital. Mr. Holmes and I are seeking to discover who is behind this before he or she succeeds."

"Is she seriously injured then? At what hospital is she? I should go to see her."

"She was poisoned and is at St. Bartholomew's. She is on the road to recovery." I replied.

"Thank God for that." After a pause he asked, "And this little demonstration? How could you come to such conclusions without knowing me?"

I clasped my hands onto my lapels and assumed a somewhat professorial stance to exude some authority. "The customizing of the floor and desk, the height of the most worn books on your shelves, even the placement of the paintings on your walls indicated your height."

"Could that not have been accounted for by a man in a wheelchair?" he asked.

"Possibly, but the wear pattern on the floor clearly indicated footprints, not wheel tracks. Also, why would a man in a wheelchair need a desk chair? The scuffing on the side closest to the desk indicated a limp of the right leg.

Finally, the placement of objects on your desktop indicated a right handed man."

"And my age? However could you guess such a thing?" he implored.

"My colleague, Mr. Holmes would never guess. Something I have not quite broken the habit of. However, in this instance there are some few hairs on the back of your chair, a portion of which are grey, and all indicating a fresh cutting. Since there is a mixture of grey and brown I presumed middle-aged rather than an elderly gentleman."

"Well, when you explain it, it seems simple enough," he grumbled. "Did you find the information you needed regarding Miss Fields?"

"Yes, Mr. Wooten was most helpful. We discovered your note advising her to draft a will and that none was as yet presently on file for her. This could prove useful in our investigation."

"Yes," he replied, "I've been meaning to remind her of that again. So many of my younger clients fail to consider the possibility of their passing. When an unexpected event occurs, their families suffer the consequences."

"Yes, the immortality of youth seems to run high in this generation."

He pondered that a moment and asked, "Is there any more I can do for you then, Doctor?"

"I believe I have sufficient information for now. Be assured I, or Mr. Holmes, will call upon you again should something else come to mind."

"Very well. Give Miss Fields my best and let her know I'll come around to see her soon."

"I shall, sir." I then turned to leave. As Mr. Wooten met me at the door with my stick and bowler I chanced to gaze again upon the nameplate with the solicitor's name and turned to face my host once more.

"By the way, Mr. Salmon" I said, pointing to the engraving. "This 'T' wouldn't happen to stand for 'Timothy' would it?"

Chapter Eleven

"You should have seen the look on his face, Holmes." I conveyed to my friend that evening as we dined at Simpson's. "I understand now, your inclination toward the dramatic at times. It was a most delicious sensation."

We had arrived at the restaurant simultaneously, which was unusual in itself. Habitually our meetings had him arriving early, but in disguise, or late, but with news that solved, or at least advanced our case. I was devouring my way through some beef Wellington and he a grilled steak, when our conversation turned toward my adventure at the law offices of Mr. T. James Salmon.

Holmes gave me one of his little half smiles and sipped his coffee. "I'm glad to see some of my lessons in observation have rubbed off on you, Doctor. But tell me, what was it, exactly, that made you deduce that his name was Timothy?"

"Ah, this is where I may have had some advantage over your methods, old fellow. When I saw his name engraved upon the door of his office it triggered a memory of my days in her majesty's service. An officer in my regiment also had a similar nameplate upon his desk. A Major T. Benjamin Gil, who preferred 'Ben' to 'Timothy'. It was actually rather a joke among us. He was known as 'Ben Gil' while we were serving in the Bengal regions of the sub-continent before our transfer to the Afghan frontier."

Holmes grimaced at this play on words.

"At any rate," I continued, "that reminded me of the fact that my regiment had an inordinate amount of men named 'Timothy' among the officers who were a few years older than I. As our lawyer friend was of this same generation, I deduced that 'Timothy' was a common name for boys born of this era, such as there have been periods of Georges, Charles, Edwards and the like. I thus made my pronouncement based on this evidence and was acknowledged as correct by Mr. Salmon's reaction."

Holmes looked at me thoughtfully and proceeded to take a cigar from his sterling case and light it. As he watched the first plumes of blue smoke drift toward the ceiling he spoke softly, "Watson, you amaze me."

Naturally, I beamed in this praise from the master of deductive reasoning. Brightly I replied, "I merely used your methods, Holmes."

He smiled as he flicked some ashes onto his plate and looked down at the table. He then turned his face toward me and pointed with the unlit end of his cigar. "Your observations were first rate, Doctor, as far as judging his height, age, right-handedness and his limp."

I modestly lowered my head as he returned the cigar to his lips. "However, having all these facts at hand, I am afraid I cannot congratulate you on how you came about his name."

I furrowed my brow and stared across the table at him. "But it was a reasonable assumption, Holmes, and it proved correct!"

"Ah, there you said it, Watson! It was an assumption, albeit based upon certain facts. However, they were facts derived outside of the evidence before you.

"His first name could just as easily have been Thomas, or Thaddeus or Theodore, all common English names. The fact that he did not advertise his name is most telling and provides a vital clue to his identity.

"Think, Watson, there are any number of reasons why a man would not use his given name. Perhaps it is the same name as an infamous criminal. Perhaps he was named after his father and wished to establish his own identity. He may have committed some embarrassing act in his youth and wished to re-establish his reputation under a different, though still legal name."[1]

I nodded and said "I agree those could all be good reasons, Holmes, but the facts are that many men of his generation are named Timothy."

"In your experienced sampling of data you found it so, Doctor. But it is a 'limited' sampling. What you need to do in such instances is continue to ask yourself 'why?' until you have a complete conclusion. Sometimes you need ask it only once and other times it may take up to five queries, but I have found that three is usually sufficient."

"I don't understand, Holmes."

He took another long pull on his cigar and exhaled a ring of smoke. "First," he said pointing to it, "you have a man unwilling to use his first name. You need to ask 'Why would any man not wish to use his given name?' Is it out of embarrassment; to avoid confusion; or does he simply just not like it? Second," he added, blowing out another ring, "you have what appears to be a generation of men his age where Timothy is a common name. Why is Timothy a common name of that generation? What was going on at that point in time and who was the Timothy these men are named for? For example, was there an evangelistic movement sweeping the country at the time and these men all named for Timothy in the Bible?

"These two factors may be totally unrelated, Watson, especially if Miss Fields' lawyer is not named Timothy.

---

[1] In Holmes's own case, his father wished to name him William Sherlock, after the 17th century theologian and author. His mother desired to call him after her favourite author, Sir Walter Scott. A compromise was reached and he was christened William Sherlock Scott Holmes. The prevailing theory as to why he is known as Sherlock is that he wished to make a name for himself and felt that both William and Scott were too common, whereas Sherlock would be remembered.

However, you have taken it as a working hypothesis to see if it fits your other facts."

I nodded and took out a cigarette to smoke as I pondered his dissertation.

Holmes blew out a third smoke ring and continued his lesson. "The last question is 'Why would Mr. Salmon, in particular, object to using this name of Timothy?' If you came up with reasonable conclusions to the previous *whys* that fit all the facts you've established, answering this third *why* may prove your hypothesis.

"So you're telling me," I stated flatly with a bit of challenge to my voice, "that you could have discerned his name from the facts at hand without the knowledge I possessed from my military service that Timothy was a common name for that generation of English youth?"

Holmes smiled and extinguished his cigar. He pushed back slightly from the table and crossed his legs, with his long hands clasped around his knee.

"There may have been another reason, such as to avoid confusion. However, his height, his age and the fact that he walks with a limp suggests that he was embarrassed by the comparison to his namesake. Especially, for a proud man serving in the legal profession. Do you recall your Dickens, Doctor?"

"I am familiar with his works, naturally. What English schoolboy isn't?" I replied.

Then it struck me like a thunderbolt! "Of course! Tiny Tim, from *A Christmas Carol!*"

Holmes gave in to that enigmatic smile of his. "Published in 1843, just shortly before your middle-aged lawyer would have been born."

"So how did you conclude embarrassment as the cause?" I asked.

"He was obviously sensitive about his height, Watson. The customization of his office floor and desk speaks volumes. Even the height of the head clerk's desk suggests that when he entered the office he didn't want to be the only one looked down upon, so he designed the entrance in such a way that *all* would have to look up to be recognized."

"Well, Holmes, you certainly seemed to have nailed it more securely than my own conclusion." I admitted, grudgingly.

"Ah, my friend, do not be downcast. All your other observations were spot on and I could not have concluded a thing without their accuracy. You are proving more valuable to me than ever.

"Now, let me tell you of my field trip to St. Albans."

Chapter Twelve

St. Albans is a rural market town in Hertfordshire, a little over twenty miles north of London. It is named for the first British Christian martyr, who was beheaded there approximately A.D. 304. In Roman times it was second in size only to London. At one time it was site of the principal abbey in England and the first draft of the Magna Carta was drawn up there. Before the railway, it was the first coach stop for travellers journeying north out of London.

Within its boundaries to the southwest, just off the road to the village of St. Stephens, one finds Chiswell Green Lane, wherein lies the home to the Royal National Rose Society.

Leaving the metropolis of London, Holmes sped along by train through the gentle slopes and fields north of the city into a beautiful day in the country. Alighting at St. Albans station in less than an hour, he hired a gig with a sprightly mare and set off for the two mile journey to Chiswell Green. Descending the slope of Holywell Hill, he turned west into Chiswell Green Lane and tied off in front of the Rose Society where a few other conveyances were also parked. Entering the grounds, Holmes walked past the circular fountain and its surrounding benches with patches of roses in various shades of yellows and pinks, and turned left into the main structure.

Herein he walked up to a stout elderly gentleman at a desk who greeted him enthusiastically.

"Good afternoon, sir." He smiled and stood "How may I be of assistance to you? A tour perhaps?"

Holmes leaned forward on his walking stick and replied in his friendliest manner. "I'm sure a tour would be delightful on this fine spring day, sir. However, I am seeking some particular knowledge and was wondering if there were an expert available who could enlighten me as to any additives that might be used on rose plants or their soil."

"Ah, you'll be wantin' to talk to Mr. Donnelly. Follow me, sir." The greeter walked slowly through the lobby at Holmes's side to the rear entrance. He opened the door upon a vista of walking paths stretching in several directions and lined with scores of varieties of roses in seemingly every size and colour.

"Mr. Donnelly will likely be back that way," he said, stretching his hand off in a south-easterly direction. "He'll either be in the greenhouse or close by. He's a stocky gentleman with brown hair and beard but no moustache. He'll have on overalls and a straw hat. You'd be hard pressed to miss him. I'd take you back myself but I'm required to stay on duty here for visitors."

Holmes smiled and saluted the man with his stick. "That's quite all right, sir. I'm sure I can find my way. Thank you!"

Setting off, Holmes walked down a path lined by knee-high rose bushes in full bloom. "The scent *was* incredible, Watson," he confessed to me. "I'd highly recommend a visit for you and your bride when she recovers. However, I was on a mission and, while the observances naturally imprinted themselves on my mind, my appreciation would have to wait for another time."

Reaching the greenhouse, Holmes found Donnelly off in a corner at a potting bench with a large wooden tub holding a rose bush with blossoms of an unusual coral colour.

As he approached he heard the man muttering to himself, "Now, now, you've got to let the kiddies grow up and live their own lives." At which point he reached for some clippers and spotted Holmes approaching.

"Good morning, good fellow!" he called out in greeting. "Come take a look at this!"

Holmes continued toward the man and enquired, "What have you there, sir?"

"Ah 'tis a new variety I'm attempting, but the parents just don't want to let go. See these suckers coming up and the cluster of buds?"

Holmes leaned in and noted that the offending branches arising from the stalk had fewer thorns and clusters of four to six small buds that were beginning to reveal a deep pink color that was no match for the beautiful coral of the larger and more separated blossoms already in bloom. "You seem to have invaders," he responded.

"Aye, occasionally one of the strains used to interbreed attempt to take over the new generation. The secret now is to clip these suckers just halfway back."

"It would not be better to remove them at the root stalk?" asked my friend.

"Oh, no!" exclaimed the venerable gardener, "That will only promote more suckers and take away from the growth of the new breed. There!" he said as he clipped the final cluster in half, "That should do for now."

Turning to face his visitor he pointed Holmes to a nearby stool and asked, "Now, young man, what can I do for you?"

Holmes took the proffered seat and removed a piece of paper from his pocket. Handing it to Donnelly he asked, "I'm curious as to whether these chemicals are normally to be found in the growing or preservation of roses."

The older gentleman removed a glove, reached out with a pudgy leathery hand and took the list.

"Hmm, yes, these are familiar to me. Do you happen to know in what proportions they were used?"

"I'm afraid my sampling was too small to be accurate." answered Holmes. "But, you say this is normal?"

"Well, I wouldn't say 'normal' quite yet," the rose expert replied. "If the proportions are correct this is a formula that was patented just a few months ago and is still in experimental stages. It's meant to make the flowers remain fresher after they are cut, so they can be enjoyed longer in arrangements. Only specific red roses are subjected to it at this time until its effects are verified."

"I see," said Holmes, taking the list back as it was handed to him. "Have there been any ill effects noted from its use?"

"Well, I've not heard of any. But this formula has only been in limited use since February. There has been a renewed interest in rose production and preservation since the Tournament of Roses was held on New Year's Day in California. Young McAllister, God rest his soul, came up with this mixture in hopes of giving his roses a longer life after cutting, so that their value would increase."

At this point I interjected. "Holmes, do you mean to say that McAllister is dead?"

"Exactly my question to Donnelly," he answered. "He affirmed that Gregory McAllister had died in April. Further questions elicited the information that his sister and brother–in-law were now running the family business and lived just down the road in St. Stephens. But let us continue this discussion back at Baker Street, for I have exhausted my supply of cigars and feel a need for a fresh pipe."

On the cab ride north to Mrs. Hudson's, he told me Donnelly had informed him McAllister had died of some form of "sclerosis". Upon receiving directions from the rose gardener, he let the gig's mare have her head and cantered briskly down Holywell Road and on to the outskirts of the village of St. Stephens. There he laid his eyes upon the verdant fields, hedges and greenhouses of the McAllister Estate.

Once ensconced back in our familiar rooms, a pipe primed with his favourite shag, he recommenced his story with his arrival at the home of our client's former suitor.

He drove in the gate, which was a rather large arbour of bougainvillea. The house was to his right. There was a sign pointing to a stall off to the left, indicating fresh flowers and plants for sale. He decided to begin his enquiries there.

The nurseryman who met Holmes as he alighted was a young man of perhaps twenty-five. He was wearing dungarees on his lanky five foot eight inch frame and a long sleeve shirt despite the warmth of the day. Leather gloves protruded from one pocket and a red bandana from another. From under a straw hat, which provided a modicum of shade over his blond hair, he greeted my friend with enthusiasm.

"Good day, sir! What can I interest you in today? Vegetables for your garden? Flowers for a fair lady? We have a wide variety of plants for your every need!"

Holmes quickly apprised the young man and said, "I have a particular interest in roses, sir. Mr. Donnelly in St. Albans recommended that you might be able to assist me."

"Well, a recommendation from Brendan Donnelly is a fine thing indeed!" he replied. "My name is Weber, Ben Weber. My wife and I run the farm for her father, Dr. McAllister."

"Yes, I had heard that his son, Gregory, had recently passed away. I was sorry to learn that."

"Yes, it was indeed a shock to us all. Especially the doctor. No father should ever have to bury his son. Ah, here's Esther now."

Coming in from a greenhouse behind the storefront, a thin young woman emerged and removed her hat, shaking out her long red hair. She wore a plain grey dress with a green striped apron. As she removed her gloves, Weber introduced her.

"This is my wife, Esther. I don't believe I caught your name, sir."

"Holmes," answered the detective with a bow, "Sherlock Holmes. I was up from London and just learned about your unfortunate brother. You have my deepest condolences."

"Thank you. Mr. Holmes, you say?" She stepped behind the counter and sat on a tall stool. "What brings you to us today?"

Holmes told of his visit to the Rose Society and how Donnelly had mentioned that her brother was the inventor of the formula being tested for rose preservation.

"Are you a florist, then?" she asked.

"More of an amateur chemist." he answered.

She pondered that statement for a moment and then said to her husband, "Ben, why don't you take Mr. Holmes back to the special section where Gregory planted his roses with his formula and show him about? I'll mind things up here."

Thus, Weber escorted Holmes to the back of the greenhouse where he explained how Gregory McAllister had experimented with a variety of chemicals until he found what he thought was the right mixture. Tests were still being run, but the results were promising.

Upon their return to the storefront they found Dr. McAllister had joined his daughter. They were both sitting behind the counter in deep discussion.

"Did you find out what you needed?" asked the woman. "My father will be glad to answer any of your questions."

Holmes looked at the white-haired doctor and repeated his earlier statement, "My condolences on the loss of your son, sir. I did have some questions about his formula if you don't mind speaking of it."

At that moment the older man, with surprising alacrity for his age, brought up a shotgun from behind the counter and aimed it straight at Holmes heart. "I'll just bet ye do," he stated flatly.

His aged, ice-blue eyes bore into Holmes like rapiers. His daughter, a pistol now in her own hand, spoke sharply, "Ben, come over here away from him."

Unhesitant but confused, the young man obeyed and implored, "Esther, Doctor, what are you doing?"

"I don't know what his game is," replied his wife, "but this man is an imposter and we'll have the truth out of him before he leaves this room."

Holmes, having been given no instructions as yet, slowly sat on the corner of a nearby table with one long leg dangling over its edge.

"Pray tell, madam," Holmes stated matter-of-factly as he folded his arms across his chest, "however did you arrive at such a conclusion?"

From behind the counter she pulled up a copy of the *Lippincott's* containing *The Sign of the Four* and waved it toward him, her voice forceful and intolerant. "Next time you try to use a phony name sir, it shouldn't be one so unusual and so recently in the public eye as a piece of fiction." She slapped the magazine on the counter. "I recognized it as soon as you said it, since I just finished reading this story last week. So who are you and what are you doing here?"

Holmes addressed me from his chair. "So you see, Watson, your legal friends aren't the only ones who find your stories so unbelievable as to be fictitious."

Defensively I replied, "Your skills are so unusual that they **are** hard to believe, Holmes. Yet, you've taken nearly no credit in any of the crimes you've solved for the police. This is only the second time you've allowed me to publish one of your adventures, and the last was three years ago[1]. If you would allow me to record more of them, people would become familiar with your work. Indeed it may even bring you more clients."

"Possibly, Doctor," Holmes replied, lighting his pipe again. "But I shudder at the prospect of everyone with their minor little problems beating a path to my door when I only seek those issues which can exercise my mind to its fullest.

"But let us return to McAllister's Farm."

---

[1] *A Study in Scarlet*, December 1887

Chapter Thirteen

Holmes glanced derisively at the magazine, then at the shotgun and finally settled on to Esther Weber's flashing green eyes.

"Mrs. Weber," he stated calmly "I assure you that everything I have told you thus far is absolutely true. There are other facts I did not wish to burden you with, but I see that I must confide the whole story to you in order to gain your trust. I must, however, ask that you not discuss any of what I'm about to tell you until I let you know the guilty parties have been apprehended."

At this point, Dr. McAllister spoke in his high-pitched Scottish brogue, "We'll make no promises to a man who lies about his own name. Tell us who ye are afore ye say another word."

"Allow me to access my wallet and show you my identification." replied Holmes.

"Aye, but no quick moves. This old shotgun would make an awful mess at this range."

Holmes smiled and slowly pulled back his left lapel until his inner pocket was in sight. Then with just two fingers, he removed his wallet and flipped it to Weber.

The young man caught it and opened it up, looking through the papers and cards.

"Well?" asked his wife, "Who is he, Ben?"

The nurseryman looked at his wife and sputtered, "There's a telegram addressed to Mr. Sherlock Holmes, 221B Baker Street, London. Several cards with the same name and address on them. A few other business cards, but no more than one of each and some currency."

"What? That's impossible!" He must have had some fake cards printed up so he could carry out this charade."

"I don't think so, Esther," her husband replied, "The telegram is dated yesterday and it's from the Royal National Rose Society, verifying the hours that they're open to the public."

"He still could have sent it under a fake name and received a reply as long as he was at that address."

"Mrs. Weber," Holmes interrupted, "I can see that you are a prudent woman and I'm sure you have concerns of the patent on your brother's formula, since it may indeed be the saving grace of this farm."

She raised the pistol barrel up so it now pointed at the ceiling. However her father's shotgun did not waver.

"You say you've just recently read Dr. Watson's story. If I may give a demonstration of his *character's* abilities would you allow that perhaps it is not a work of fiction, as you suppose?"

"And how do you propose to do that?"

"Let us start with your husband, who is not a nurseryman by trade, but rather a bookkeeper. He has taken up this work to supplement your brother's absence. You, on the other hand, have spent frequent time in the outdoors and prefer horseback riding and gardening to the society life of a young woman of means."

She slowly lowered the gun to her waist as Holmes continued, it now pointed toward the floor, but by no means lax should it be needed.

"Doctor McAllister," Holmes said softly, looking into the wary eyes, "I'm sorry to see you have suffered a medical condition which eliminates your ability to perform surgery and reduced your practice to consulting. I would imagine the loss of patients from a doctor who can't heal himself must be extremely frustrating to a man of your calibre. Incidentally, I thank you for not cocking that shotgun. I'm sure a doctor sworn to 'do no harm' would be devastated by an accidental discharge where none was intended. Am I correct in deducing the early onset of Parkinson's disease?"

The doctor seemed to relax. He turned the shotgun aside, set it on the counter and sat back down. His daughter let her hand with the pistol fall to her side and Weber returned Holmes wallet, asking "How did you know I was a bookkeeper, Mr. Holmes?"

"The calluses on your fingers are those of one accustomed to writing, not handling garden tools. Your fair skin and the peeling of sunburn from your neck indicate you are not yet acclimated to outdoor work in bright sunlight, which I gather is also the reason for your long sleeves on this warm day."

"That is all true, sir. I have been the bookkeeper here for four years and just took to helping out when we lost Gregory."

"Mr. Holmes," declared Mrs. Weber, "you have indeed lived up to Dr. Watson's writings. I did not believe such skills could actually exist. Could you explain your conclusions about me?"

"Dr. Watson tends to dramatize and romanticize what should have been a textbook lesson in the science of deduction," the detective groused, "However, in your case, if you will note your own hands, the skin surely shows a toughening where you would hold a horse's reins. You have the natural bearing of an experienced horsewoman and I noted a young chestnut stallion in the corral with the draught animals for your wagons, which would appear to be a perfect size for you. With your sleeves rolled up as they are, I can note that your skin tone, though fair, shows signs of many years exposure to the sun which reduces your susceptibility to burning.

"From the greenhouse there is an open doorway to the barn where I noted four saddles, two of which are dusty and need conditioning. None of them were sidesaddles, by which I determine that you are a woman who likes a spirited animal and needs to ride astride to have better control of it. This is not the normal practice of young society ladies and I sensed a no-nonsense aspect to your personality when we were introduced. You do not succumb easily to flattery and prefer straight talk and intellectual discussion to flightiness and gossip."

"This is amazing, Mr. Holmes," cried the doctor. "Ye have described Esther as if you've known her for years."

"Observation and deduction. As I'm sure you practise in your own profession."

"Aye, when I had a profession. Ye were right about that too. The Parkinson's has caused my practice to dwindle and the farm had a bad year last year. Gregory's formula may be our salvation, so we are naturally very protective of it."

Holmes inclined his head to the older gentleman. "I assure you, sir, that my interest is purely in regard to a case I have in hand."

"Well then," replied the senior McAllister, picking up the shotgun and slinging it over his shoulder, "let us be off to the house for some refreshment and we'll see how we can help ye."

* * *

At the conclusion of Holmes's story McAllister sat back in his chair and ran his fingers through his white hair.

"That's an amazin' tale, Mr. Holmes. Gregory was always smitten by that actress and looked for her again after he'd finished up his time at sea. That must have been when she changed her name 'cause he never did find her again."

"Good riddance, I said," piped up Esther Weber. "Those theatre folk are not ones to be involved with. His pining over her made him pass up more than one chance at a good marriage."

"I do not know what sort of companion she would have made your son, Doctor," replied Holmes, "but she needs help now. You've verified the formula ingredients for me and I need not know their proportions so you can keep that secret safe for your patent. What I do need are two things."

"Whatever we can do, Mr. Holmes," said McAllister.

"Whatever else she may be, she's a woman in distress," responded his daughter with a reluctant sigh. "What do you need?"

Holmes folded his long fingers together and replied, "First I need to know if anyone has reported any ill effects from exposure to the formula. Either through handling it or, perhaps, from a puncture wound sustained from a rose that was treated with it."

The doctor shook his head. "There's been nothing like that ever been told to us. We've all handled it with no problems and our clients and customers have not reported any such incident."

"Very well," said the detective, "All the better for you if it's safe. The other thing I need is a list of your London clients. Dr. Watson has not yet found the florist who delivered them or who put together any such lily and rose arrangement."

"That I can get for you, Mr. Holmes," and Gregory McAllister's sister left the room momentarily to return and hand Holmes a multi-page brochure.

"These are all arrangements Gregory came up with to recommend to our florist clients who are listed on the back. They're all either in Covent Garden, Marylebone or Westminster. There is the arrangement you mentioned. It was the first my brother came up with. Oddly enough, inspired by his memory of Miss Fields."

Holmes studied the picture and noted the name of the arrangement. *Song of Songs 2:2.*

"Do you know your scripture, Mr. Holmes?" asked the doctor.

"I'm afraid this verse eludes me, sir," he replied.

Clearing his throat the doctor recited "As a lily among the thorns, so is my Darling among the maidens."

Chapter Fourteen

"So, Watson," Holmes intoned as he tapped out his pipe, "if you would be so kind as to take this list of the McAllister clients and see if you can determine our flower sender, I shall be most grateful."

Reaching out and taking the brochure from his hand, I glanced at it and determined that the location of most of these establishments was nearer to my home than the ones I had previously sought out between the theatre and St. Bartholomew's.

Noting the time, I stood and retrieved my hat and stick, "Very well, Holmes, I shall begin my enquiries first thing in the morning. What plans have you for tomorrow?"

"I shall explore along the threads of what you discovered at our diminutive solicitor's and see if a pattern emerges. Have a good night, my friend."

The next morning, I arose early and enjoyed a light breakfast. Afterward, I set out upon the route that would be most advantageous for checking out each of the clients on the McAllister list. While a few of the shops I first contacted had, indeed, sent out the *Song of Songs* arrangement in the past month, none of those were destined for the Lyceum Theatre.

After six such shops I found myself, just before noon, near the Criterion Bar. I had encountered Stamford there years ago, which led to my introduction to Holmes. I thought I would stop in for a bite and found that the next shop on my list was just a few doors down. Putting off my meal for a few more minutes, I entered and was waited upon by a lovely young lady with wavy brown hair and dark brown eyes.

"Hello sir!" she exclaimed. "My name's Rozzy, how can I help you?"

I introduced myself and explained, for the seventh time, that I was seeking information about the *Song of Songs* arrangements that had been sent to the Lyceum theatre for the past several Saturdays.

To my relief, she brightened and stated, "Oh yes! I put those arrangements together myself. In fact I did another one this morning, but this was sent to a patient at St. Bartholomew's Hospital."

Instantly alert, I asked, "Would that patient be Loraine Fontaine?"

"Why, yes, Doctor!" she marvelled.

"Who sent them?" I pleaded.

"He didn't leave his name. Just ordered up that arrangement and told me who and where they were to be delivered to."

"Oh," I stated dejectedly, and then thought, "Can you describe him for me?"

"Well, he must have been in his late twenties, a handsome man, about your height but thinner. He had brown hair, rather long. He had a very nice voice and was very polite."

"I see," I said, making notes in my notebook, "Anything else?"

"Hmm, ah! He was left-handed. I noticed when he made out the card for the flowers."

I brightened at that fact and continued, "But you did not see him sign his name?" I asked.

"Oh, no sir. We give them an envelope to put the card in. He paid his bill and went on his way. That was about ten o'clock this morning."

"And was this the same man who ordered the arrangements that went to the Lyceum Theatre?"

"That I don't know. All those arrangements were ordered by mail and they went to a different person."

"What? Who?" I asked.

She reached under the counter and brought out a box of papers. Soon she held the letter in her hand.

"Those arrangements went to Lily Harley."

"Miss Harley?" I asked, bewildered by this revelation.

"Yes, Doctor. The letters arrived with a bank draft for payment and my brother, Roger, delivered them at ten o'clock every Saturday night for several weeks now."

"If there was a bank draft then you must know who ordered these arrangements." I stated hopefully.

"Yes," she read," these were ordered by Mr. Charles Chaplin of Liverpool."

* * *

I pondered this information over a quick lunch at the Criterion and then hailed a cab for St. Bart's, where I found my wife and Miss Fontaine chattering away over the latest delivery of flowers.

"John!" my wife exclaimed upon my appearance in the doorway, "Look what arrived this morning."

The *Song of Songs* arrangement brightened the room from a vase by the window. Like the others, it held one dozen red roses surrounding a single white lily.

Kissing Mary's cheek, I sat and told them my discovery at the last florist I visited.

"Did the card arrive with these?" I asked.

111

"Yes." replied Miss Fontaine, "But it still is of no help."

She handed it to me and I read:

> *As the lily stands among the thorns*
> *So may you, the stage soon adorn.*
> *Well wishes for a rapid recovery.*
>
> *An Admirer*

"As you can see, Doctor," continued the actress, "these could have come from anyone."

"But in fact," I stated "We know that the flowers that were delivered to the theatre were for Lily Harley from Charles Chaplin."

"But then how did they come to be delivered to me?"

"The gentleman who ordered these flowers," I said, pointing at the arrangement, "was in his late twenties, my height but thinner with long brown hair and he was left-handed. Does that suggest anyone to you?"

My wife's friend pondered for a moment, but shook her head. "No one comes to mind, Doctor."

"John," said Mary, "that sounds like the man who drove us here on the night Lilly took ill."

"Exactly, my dear," I replied, patting her hand. "That man also sounds like the same man who told Figgins that the flowers each Saturday were for Miss Fontaine."

"Who was that?" enquired the actress.

"The singer, Leo Dryden."

"Leo? Why would he divert flowers meant for Lily to me?" enquired the actress.

"That is indeed a question," I replied. "Especially in light of the fact that my information indicates that he may have romantic feelings for Miss Harley."

"Why, John," responded Mary, "that much is obvious. Whoever this Charles Chaplin is, he must be a rival for Miss Harley's affections."

"Perhaps so," I agreed, "But then why *this* arrangement to Miss Fontaine?"

"That may be a puzzle for Mr. Holmes," she answered. "On the other hand," she continued thoughtfully, "perhaps you and I can follow up on that."

"What are you suggesting, Mary?" I asked sceptically.

"Well, now that Constable MacDonald is on nightly duty here, and the nurses keep giving me looks like, *'Why is she still here?'*, perhaps it's time for me to get out and help you and Mr. Holmes."

I started to protest but then saw *that* look in her eye and decided, for the better part of valour, that perhaps I could use some help.

Chapter Fifteen

However, before allowing Mary to leave the hospital, I felt it necessary to inform her of the heart murmur that Eckstein had found. I took her off to a quiet place alone to discuss this.

When I had finished giving her the news, she sat quietly for some time. We hugged and she let out one brief sob. Then, with that resolve I've witnessed so often, she straightened up and said, "Well, then we'll just have to make the best of it. It's never bothered me before and now that we know it's there we'll just have to take appropriate precautions."

Consulting with Dr. Kennedy, we agreed that he would run another test on Mary's heart and, if all went well, she could leave that evening. In the meantime, I was to go by Baker Street and then home to fetch Mary some proper clothing for her departure.

Arriving at Mrs. Hudson's, I ascended the stairs and found, as I supposed, that my friend was not in. I sat at the desk and was writing out an explanation of all I had learned that day when Mrs. Hudson's cherubic face appeared at the door.

"Good afternoon, Doctor," she smiled. "Mr. Holmes left this note for you. He said he would not likely be back until tomorrow or the next day."

I thanked her and accepted the note from her hand. It read:

I finished my note and left it in the Persian slipper with his tobacco. I could not trust its presence to be noticed on his perpetually untidy desk. Deeming that my information regarding the flowers was not urgent, I forbore telegraphing him. I pointed out my note to Mrs. Hudson should he return and continued my journey home to retrieve my wife's necessities.

Our maid, Ivy, assisted me in putting together a carpetbag of my wife's things and I made off again for St. Bartholomew's. With the doctor's tests confirming her health and MacDonald's presence accounted for, Mary bade good evening to her friend and promised daily visits until her recovery.

We stepped out to the street. I hailed a cab and enquired whether my bride would prefer to go straight home or stop somewhere for dinner.

Patting my hand she replied, "I'm sure you would much prefer a restaurant to Ivy's cooking tonight, John. And I believe I'd like to stop by the Lyceum after dinner. Can we get in backstage?"

I assured her that both the stage manager and the door guard were acquainted with our investigation and we should have no trouble.

"Are you sure you are ready for all this activity, darling? Three days of bed rest isn't always easy to recover from," I posed.

"I'm fine, my Love," she responded. "Now tell me, what has Mr. Holmes been up to?"

I explained Holmes's trip to St. Albans and his discoveries there.

"Poor Gregory, never finding his true love," my wife lamented. "All those years wasted."

"Certainly not as lucky as we are," I replied, interlacing her fingers in mine.

She smiled and gave me a quick discreet kiss on the cheek.

"Should we tell Lilly?" she asked.

"As a doctor I would recommend waiting until she has completely recovered. If this news were to cause her any remorse it could lead to depression which she should avoid at all costs right now."

"What about the flowers? Is she in any danger from them?"

"Apparently the chemicals in the flowers have not caused any problems with anyone else," I concluded. "Therefore, it must have been the poison in the milk that caused Miss Fontaine's illness."

"But my symptoms were different, John. How could that be?"

"I can't be sure until I learn what chemicals Holmes found, but it probably had to do with your heart condition."

She pondered that. "My 'heart condition'. What a dreadful term! I'm much too young for such a thing."

"Many people are born with heart issues that are never found until it's too late, my Love. We're lucky we caught this now and can treat it accordingly."

"Oh, I suppose," she sighed, taking my arm and leaning on me as the cab rolled through the streets toward the theatre district. "But don't you go treating me with any kid gloves, Doctor or I'll have to show you just how tough I can be!"

We continued on in silence, each lost in our own thoughts, until we spotted a small restaurant not far from the Lyceum and had the cab driver pull up there to enjoy a delicious dinner.

* * *

117

Forging on to the theatre, we arrived at the rear entrance where Mr. Washburn passed us through with a nod and a smile. We wove our way among the actors and props, for Mary was determined to meet Leo Dryden. Upon reaching the dressing area where he kept his table, we found it vacant. This was not altogether surprising as his performance for the day should have been concluded. The main attraction was now occurring on stage.

"Let's head down to the wings," I offered. "He may well be watching Miss Harley's performance from there."

"I wouldn't be surprised," Mary answered. "There's something strange going on here and I believe it would be most helpful to Mr. Holmes's investigation if we can sort it out."

Approaching the wings on stage right, we could see actors coming and going from the play according to their cues, but no sign of the singing comic. As we weren't able to close in without being in the way, I could not determine if he, perhaps, was over in the stage left wings instead. At that moment, chance brought Mr. Figgins across our path and I entreated him as to the whereabouts of the elusive Mr. Dryden.

"Have you not heard then, Doctor?" he answered. "Leo Dryden was arrested this afternoon, right after his matinee performance!"

* * *

As Figgins was engaged in managing the production in progress, he could not take the time to give us particulars. He suggested we go upstairs to Mr. Irving's office, as the owner was present when Scotland Yard made the arrest.

With some little difficulty, we managed to find our way to the producer's suite and found Irving going over paperwork with another man. Seeing us in his doorway, he dismissed the fellow and invited us in.

"Doctor! Please come in and sit down," he bellowed, "And who is this vision of beauty whom you have brought in to brighten my office?"

I introduced Mary and he gallantly took her hand and bowed. "A pity then," he remarked, and quickly explained himself. "Forgive my phrasing, Mrs. Watson, I merely meant that a woman of your attraction and bearing has the possibilities of a stage career. I am always seeking new talent."

"No offence taken, Mr. Irving, thank you," Mary answered. "But we've come on another matter regarding my friend, Lilly... that is, Loraine Fontaine."

"Ah, yes!" he smiled broadly, "Well, we've good news there. Inspector Lestrade was here this afternoon and arrested Leo Dryden. I was surprised that our friend Holmes had not beaten the Yard to the punch this time."

"Holmes is pursuing another lead," I answered. "What did Lestrade have to say?"

"Oh, he is quite convinced that Dryden is our man. Something about being left-handed, having access to the milk where the poison was inserted and such."

"Did he offer a motive for Dryden's action?" asked Mary.

"He was not specific, Mrs. Watson. But he seemed quite sure of himself," replied the theatre owner. "A pity to lose Dryden. He was a good draw, if not quite star quality."

I spoke up, perhaps a little defensively, for I could not quite believe that Holmes could be easily beaten by the *official* police. I also may have held myself somewhat accountable for not following up the Dryden connection with more vigour, so that Holmes could have all the facts. "Lestrade has been 'quite sure of himself' on several occasions, Mr. Irving, where, in the end, his conclusions proved entirely erroneous."

"Well, we shall see, Doctor. I hope he is right though, and that this is the end of Miss Fointaine's troubles."

We bid our host farewell and, over Mary's protests, I hailed a cab to take us home. She had desires to go to Scotland Yard and speak with Dryden herself, for she was not convinced that Lilly was out of danger.

"You need to get to bed, my Love. As a physician, as well as your husband, I insist that you not overtax yourself," I reasoned. "It's not likely we could see Dryden tonight anyway. I'm sure Lestrade will permit us access tomorrow morning. Lilly is safe enough for tonight with MacDonald on duty."

"Very well, *Doctor!*" she replied "But promise me, tomorrow, right after breakfast, we go straight to the Yard."

"I promise, Darling." I said, taking her hand and helping her into the hansom.

With a brief stop at the telegraph office to dash off the news to William Scott – otherwise Sherlock Holmes – we proceeded to our cosy home and a peaceful night's rest in our own bed.

Chapter Sixteen

The next day, Wednesday, found us en route to Scotland Yard after a light breakfast. The fog was lifting in the promising warmth of an early summer. Even at that hour the humid smell of the Thames rose up from beyond the walls where the Yard backed up against London's famous waterway.

The hansom dropped us off about 9:30. Mary and I entered the newly built establishment, noting that some construction, even yet, was not completed. Workmen strolled about as freely as the police officers themselves.

We soon elicited directions to Lestrade's office. The Inspector was at his desk, surrounded by boxes of files and other sundry materials, looking somewhat harried.

"Ah, good morning, Dr. Watson, Mrs. Watson! I apologize for the mess, but apparently there's been some mix up in the delivery of our filing cabinets from the old Yard. I'm afraid I'm missing my visitor chairs as well. Won't you sit down here, Mrs. Watson?" he said, offering my wife his own chair.

"How are you feeling? Can I offer you some tea or water? That was a nasty business with that poison and all."

"I'm quite fine, Inspector, thank you for asking," replied my Mary as she sat.

"Well, we've got the blackguard that did it and I assure you that justice will be done to Mr. Leo Dryden. I'm a bit surprised not to see our friend, Mr. Holmes with you. I suppose he may be a bit put off that we beat him to the capture this time."

"Mr. Holmes is out of town at the moment," I replied. Hoping to draw him out and gain information for Holmes, I appealed to the man's pride, "How did you arrive at your arrest, Inspector? I'm sure Miss Fontaine will be most interested in your story."

Beaming with self-satisfaction the bulldog detective smiled and launched into his accounting.

"I must admit Mr. Holmes did put us on the right track when he noted the left-handedness of the suspect. Dryden is, of course, a left-handed man. He had ample opportunities to slip poison into the milk that Miss Fontaine consumed regularly, what with it being a public icebox. We found that poison in the milk, still in the jug in the tea service. Our laboratory is not yet running at full efficiency and hasn't had time to identify the type of poison yet."

"Forgive me, Inspector," asked Mary, "but what was Dryden's motive?"

"Ah, Mrs. Watson, I see your marriage to the doctor has indoctrinated you into the ways of criminology. His motive is one of the oldest there is. Love."

"Love?" I responded, feigning ignorance at the rumours I had heard.

"Oh yes, Doctor. Love. It appears our friend, Dryden, is quite taken by Miss Lily Harley, the understudy. He has been seen in her company on several occasions and as he is a singer and not an actor, his feelings were quite obvious to those who noticed."

Mary then remarked, "And he poisoned the star so his love interest could get the role?"

"That's our case, Mrs. Watson. Of course he denies it. Says that Miss Harley is a married woman and his interest is only friendship for a fellow actor."

"Where did he obtain the poison?" I asked.

"Oh, we'll find that out eventually, Doctor," he smirked. "Have no fear on that score!"

"May I see Mr. Dryden, Inspector?" Mary suddenly asked.

Lestrade hesitated a moment, then acquiesced. "It's a bit irregular, but I suppose if anyone has a right it would be you or Miss Fontaine. Come with me."

We made our way through the maze of construction workers and moving men and finally emerged among the prison area. Accompanied by Lestrade and a constable on guard duty, we soon found ourselves nearing Dryden's cell.

"May I speak with him alone, Inspector Lestrade?" my wife asked.

"I'm afraid that privilege is only allowed his lawyer," he answered. "Anything he says to anyone else may still be used in court against him, so there must be an officer present during any interviews."

"Lestrade, if I may make a suggestion?" I posed. "I believe Mary may be able to gain information into this love angle where a man might not be successful. Could you arrange for a female officer to accompany her while we wait?"

"Hmm, I suppose that would be worth a try. He might more easily let something slip to a woman. Wait here."

The inspector moved off and soon returned with a female officer.

"This is Miss Brooke, Dr. Watson and Mrs. Watson," Lestrade said by way of introduction.

The young woman took my wife's hand and nodded. "A pleasure, Mrs. Watson. Doctor, I have found your tales of Sherlock Holmes to be most illuminating. I should like to meet him someday to discuss his methods."

"I'm sure that can be arranged," I replied. "Thank you for helping us in our little situation here."

"Anything to serve justice. Shall we go in, Mrs. Watson?"

Upon their entrance into the cell holding the singing comic he stood and bowed slightly.

"Ladies, what can I do for you? Wait, don't I know you? Were you not with Miss Fontaine when I drove you all to the hospital last Saturday?"

"Yes, indeed," replied Mary. "I am Mrs. Watson. I was helping my husband and my friend when you drove us to St.

Bartholomew's. But I must warn you, that before we proceed, Miss Brooke is a detective and anything you say may be used against you in court."

"If the truth can convict an innocent man, then justice is truly blind," he replied. "I'm afraid there's not much in the way of accommodation here, but if one of you would take the chair and the other sit on the bed, I shall stand and tell you what I can."

Miss Brooke immediately moved to the bed so that my wife could take the chair.

"You understand that you are charged with the attempted murder of Lorraine Fontaine and with poisoning Mrs. Watson here, as well." began the Detective.

"Yes, yes," replied Dryden impatiently. "Your Inspector Lestrade has made that all quite clear, as absurd as the charges are."

"Are you aware that Sherlock Holmes is working on the case?" Mary countered.

"Ah well, there is some hope in that, if his reputation is justified."

"I assure you, sir, that Mr. Holmes will not rest until he is satisfied justice is done," Mary insisted. "However, you must see how it looks from the police perspective. You had access to the milk, you are left-handed, you made a wrong turn on the way to the hospital, thus delaying treatment for Miss Fontaine...."

"The wrong turn was purely accidental." he interrupted, "I'm a singer, not a cabby. I merely mistook a landmark in the dark and turned up the wrong street."

"And," continued Mary, "you have the motive of your feelings for Miss Harley."

"Leave Miss Harley out of this!" he cried. Then, realizing his emotions could betray him, he lowered his voice. "She has nothing to do with any of this. I don't know who poisoned Fontaine or why, but it was not I!"

"Then please explain why you would divert flowers meant for Miss Harley to be delivered to Miss Fontaine."

This revelation caught the man completely off guard.

"How did you ... who told you?" He stammered. He leaned back against the wall and raised his eyes to the ceiling, closed them for an instant and looked directly at my wife.

"Very well, I see I must lay my case before you in regard to Miss Harley. Perhaps as a woman you will understand.

"It's true that I have come to have very strong feelings for her. But not strong enough to kill for her success. Any anger I have in her regard is toward her husband."

"Her husband?" my wife asked innocently, although I had informed her of Holmes interview with Miss Harley.

"Yes, that drunken lout she's married to. I should explain that Lily Harley is her stage name. Her real name is Hannah Chaplin. Her husband, Charles, sent the flowers, though God knows he hasn't sent her any money to live on since he left for Liverpool. The man can't hold his liquor and so he can't hold a job. No theatre in London will take a chance on him any more. He ran off to try his luck in Liverpool, leaving her with two sons to care for and provide her own income to make ends meet. I've struck up a friendship with her that has developed into feelings of love, but I have not expressed that to her as yet. I've been waiting until the end of this production run to see if I dare approach her with the idea of divorcing him and marrying me.

"In the meantime the flowers began showing up a few weeks ago. I was fortunate enough to have been in a position to intercept the first batch and have been on guard ever since. I don't want her to fall for his line again when I can offer her so much more."

"But why the flowers yesterday, to Lorraine at the hospital?" my wife enquired.

"I'm not sure I thought that through. My intent was that I had started a ruse and felt a true admirer would keep sending the flowers. Should any more arrive at the theatre I would have intercepted them outside and disposed of them."

"Your devotion is admirable." Mary replied "More than devotion however, I would think, that honesty must win the day, for her sake, as well as your own. Suppose your plan works and later she finds out that you intercepted the flowers her husband sent? Will she not resent you for your subterfuge and never fully trust you again?"

"I'm afraid that thought did not occur to me," he admitted.

"I've only one more question," Mary continued.

"Whatever I can tell you, Mrs. Watson."

"Do you have any thoughts as to who might really have poisoned the milk?"

"Then you believe my innocence?"

"I do," replied my wife. "However," she said, looking at the detective, "Scotland Yard may need more convincing than my own intuition."

"As long as I know that you believe me and that Mr. Holmes is searching for the truth, I can retain my hopes. As to who poisoned the milk, I cannot say. However, there is that dispute between Lionel Ferguson and Harrison Colby. Colby certainly has the theatrical connections to plant someone within our ranks at the Lyceum. I suppose he would be my choice for a primary suspect."

"Thank you, Mr. Dryden. I hope that when next we meet it will be when we are applauding one of your performances."

"Will you say anything to Miss Harley?" he asked with pleading eyes.

"That I will leave to you and your conscience," she replied "I only hope you will heed my advice."

"Thank you, Mrs. Watson. God bless you."

He moved toward her, offering his hand. Miss Brooke was immediately on her feet ready to come to my wife's defence, but he only helped her rise from her chair and watched as they both exited the cell.

Duty bound as she was, Brooke reported Dryden's confession of feelings toward Lily Harley, which made the Inspector smirk in delight.

"That confirms our theory for motive then. Well done, Mrs. Watson!"

"On the contrary, Inspector," my wife replied, "Dryden may be a lovesick fool but he's no killer. In addition, there's still no accounting for the poison."

"He could have obtained that anywhere," responded Lestrade. "Oh, we've got our man all right. We'll have this wrapped up by the end of the week."

Bidding our farewells, we left the Inspector's office and returned to our home in Kensington.

Chapter Seventeen

Home found me with patients in my waiting room and a telegram from Holmes on my desk. It read:

> *Singer suspect inconclusive. Client must avoid roses. May need you tomorrow.*
>
> *Scott*

"John," Mary said, "I should go to the hospital and warn Lilly not to touch the roses."

"Are you sure you're up to it?" I replied. "I could go or we could send a telegram."

"I can get there faster than a telegram and you need to see to your patients. I feel fine." She kissed me and was out hailing a cab before I could utter another word.

For me, the rest of the morning and early afternoon was a flurry of colds, coughs, broken fingers and dislocated joints. Not to mention the inevitable hypochondriac.

Mary, on the other hand, found herself in a most interesting scenario upon her arrival at St. Bartolomew's.

Walking into Miss Fields' room, she was met by the sight of Caroline pouring milk for her mistress, while the small dark figure of a man was standing by, attempting to hand a bouquet of roses to the prostrate actress.

"Good morning, *Loraine*!" announced Mary from the doorway. The actress beamed in recognition and the gentleman looked sharply at her as she walked in, surprised by the interruption.

"Mary, how good of you to come. This," she stated by way of introduction, "is Mr. Harrison Colby. Mr. Colby, this is Mrs. Mary Watson, a very dear old friend."

Colby bowed, "A pleasure, Mrs. Watson. I was just dropping by to see how our friend was doing."

"And you brought flowers, how thoughtful," my wife replied. "Here let me put them up for you, there's space over on the window sill." Deftly she retrieved them from Colby's hand and got them away from the actress.

"Caroline," she continued as she returned, "that isn't milk from the theatre is it?"

"Oh no, Mrs. Watson. This here is fresh from the dairy. I picked it up this morning."

"Excellent, my dear! That was very thoughtful of you."

Colby cleared his throat and spoke. "As I was about to suggest, Miss Fontaine, I hope that upon your recovery you might re-consider your obligation to work in a play for me. I assure you that I have decided to move my theatrical endeavors to more legitimate engagements that would be worthy of an actress of your calibre."

"I find your reputation does not make that seem likely," replied the actress as she sipped her milk.

"Yes, I was afraid that would be your reaction. Especially considering how Ferguson feels about me. I wish I could explain to all of you about the change of heart I have had recently."

"What would that be?" enquired Mary.

"It is rather personal, Mrs. Watson, but to put it briefly, I've had a religious experience and plan to either divest or revamp my theatres to reflect a more positive cultural influence on London society."

Three pairs of feminine eyes turned toward the man in either scepticism or wonder.

"I know. I'm still adjusting to the idea myself. But let me leave you with this thought, Miss Fontaine. As you hear news of my theatrical enterprises changing, will you at least consider my proposal for a future engagement?"

"Why, Mr. Colby, I hardly know what to say. However, if evidence comes to bear and my career path allows, I can assure you that I would consider any *legitimate* offer."

"That is all I ask, dear lady. I shall keep you apprised of my future productions to prove my sincerity. Godspeed for a swift recovery. Good day, ladies."

He donned his silk hat, retrieved his walking stick and exited the room with a bow and a flourish.

"Well, that was certainly unexpected," reflected the actress.

"Yes, indeed," replied Mary. "Lilly, one of the reasons I came by was that Mr. Holmes wired us to warn you to stay away from roses. Apparently he thinks there could still be some ill effect from them."

"Really? Well, it's good we're keeping them all over by the window."

"I also have found out a little more about the roses you were getting and what Mr. Dryden was up to."

Mary went on to explain our trip to Scotland Yard that morning and her subsequent interview with Dryden. She spent a good deal of time with her friend and it was late afternoon before she returned to our home. I immediately packed her off to bed for a nap after such a rigorous first day out of hospital.

Shortly after the last of my patients had left my consulting room early that evening, the bell rang one last time. This, however, was the delivery of another message from Holmes.

This time his request was for me to travel to a certain address in Gower Street near the British Museum. There I was to meet a Mr. Bailey at 11:00 a.m. who would provide a trunk that I was to take to Holmes on the 1:00 p.m. train from St. Pancras.

The next morning, after assuring that my Mary was quite all right, I arranged for Dr. Anstruther to cover my patients and set off for Gower Street.

131

The address turned out to be that of a photography studio. At precisely 11:00 a.m., I walked through the door of this establishment. Bailey was a tall lean gentleman with wavy brown hair and a slow manner of speech.

"Dr. Watson, I presume?" he pronounced. When I nodded my acknowledgement he continued, "Yes, yes of course you are. Mr. Holmes said to expect you at eleven and here it is, eleven o'clock sharp. Well, then let's get to it. I have my equipment over here."

As he led the way to one side of the studio where he had a camera and lights and backdrops all set up, I felt it necessary to inform him that Holmes had not enlightened me as to my purpose here.

"Oh, he didn't tell you? Well, I suppose that makes sense, telegrams charging per word and all, why write the instructions twice when I can just tell you in person. That's Holmes, all right. Always a man for an economy of words."

"So, what is our purpose here today?" I asked the photographer.

"Oh, it's quite simple, yes quite simple indeed. I'm to teach you everything I can about photography between now and the time you must leave for your train. You are then to take a trunk full of my equipment with you so as to take some photographs for Mr. Holmes."

The lesson went by far too rapidly, but I took copious notes. Suddenly the time was upon us for my departure.

Taking my leave of Mr. Bailey, with his hearty good wishes, I departed for St. Pancras station.

The train passed quickly through the outskirts of northeast London. Soon I was alighting at the station closest to Woodside Park where Holmes, met me with a hearty hail. We bundled ourselves and the trunk off, via cab, to Glenlyn House. En route he explained part of his plan.

"I've engaged the room across from mine for you, Watson. For our purposes you are James Wilson, photographer, representing the National Telephone Company. Your assignment is to take photographs of local businesses for inclusion in a Telephone Directory. The company will be offering this directory for sale with the installation of its phone service later this year."

"I see," I said, not really seeing at all. "Just what does this have to do with our case?"

"Ah, that's just it, Watson. It could have everything to do with our case, or nothing could come of it whatsoever. But here we are. While you check in, I'll procure us a table at the restaurant, for I fear my timing has caused you to miss lunch. I cannot have your growling stomach spoiling your facade. I'll meet you there in ten minutes."

Over a late lunch, Holmes explained that he had been out to the manor house where Henshaw had moved in upon his marriage with our client's mother. He had timed his visit for an opportunity to see Mrs. Henshaw at an hour when her husband would be away at work. A maid had answered the door and allowed him to wait in the hall. The housekeeper came in presently and brusquely informed him Mrs. Henshaw was not currently in residence and was not expected back for some weeks. With this news, he excused himself and decided to concentrate his efforts on Mr. Henshaw, which was also part of his itinerary for this visit to the country.

"The proceeds from the estate have been failing him, Watson. That much I have been able to learn. He returned to his profession as an apothecary at a local shop earlier this year to make ends meet."

"Well," I replied, "that would certainly give him access to various poisons, the missing link in the case against Dryden. Is it possible that they could have been working together?"

"An avenue we must explore, my friend. But his wife could equally be involved, as well. That could explain her absence. However, there was an interesting development when I left the Henshaw estate. It seems there were two men on bicycles who entered the grounds just as I was on my way out. They're staying here at the hotel. Thus far my efforts to discover their business have proved fruitless, as they are being very secretive."

"Do you suspect them to be involved in Miss Fontaine's case?" I asked.

"I shall certainly consider it until I get some answers, my friend. But tell me, how did your meeting with Dryden progress? Lestrade did let you see him?"

I explained to Holmes that we did indeed pay a visit to the suspect at Scotland Yard, and how Mary had come up with the plan to interview him. Holmes was delighted at this aspect and welcomed Mary's discovery and conclusions.

"Your most excellent wife has proven her instincts again, Watson. My own plan should be able to prove whether her intuition is accurate or not."

"By the way," I asked, "why did you warn us not to allow flowers near Miss Fontaine?"

"Just a precaution, Watson. In her weakened state, another exposure to McAllister's chemicals could cause a relapse. She should be fine once the initial poison is completely out of her system."

While I continued to devour my late lunch of roast beef, Holmes explained how my role as photographer was to be played out.

Four o'clock found us in the offices of Francis O'Malley, a local businessman who owned several shops about the town, including the pharmacy shop where Henshaw worked.

Holmes introduced us as representatives of the National Telephone Company, which excited O'Malley. His corpulent frame rose from his seat, threatening to bring the armchair with it, and he rounded his desk to shake our hands in welcome.

"Oh this is grand, grand!" he exclaimed. "I can see the telephone as a great boon to business! Oh yes, a great boon indeed, gentlemen. The ability to place orders with my suppliers instantaneously, and the same for customers who wish to contact my businesses for their own merchandise. Patients calling doctors for emergencies, citizens calling for firemen when conflagrations arise. It will be a marvel, gentlemen!"

134

"Yes, indeed," responded Holmes, hoping to stem the effusiveness of Mr. O'Malley's rhetoric, so that we could state our purpose. "Which is why we've come to you first, Mr. O'Malley. We want to make it convenient for people to make those calls. We're here about our intent to publish a directory of business telephone exchanges."

"Ah, capital, capital!" cried the entrepreneur. "How can I be of assistance?"

"What we are proposing," answered Holmes, "is to take photographs of various businesses to include in our directory. As the owner of four such businesses in town you seemed the logical starting point for our endeavour."

"Ah, I see," he responded, more warily. "I assume there will be some sort of fee for this service."

Holmes glanced at me with that fleeting smile of his and announced to our host,

"Absolutely nothing for you, sir."

"Nothing?" he queried, incredulously.

"Not a single shilling, Mr. O'Malley. It will be absolutely free of charge to you."

"Free?" he repeated, suspiciously. "Gentlemen I've been in business too long to expect anything to be free. What is your advantage?"

"To be absolutely frank, Mr. O'Malley," continued Holmes, leaning back in his chair, "yours will be the only business receiving this service at no charge. By having your agreement as our first client in this area, we hope to convince the others to join in and of course, they will be charged for it. Your reputation as a successful businessman, a *forward thinking* businessman, will be our ticket to signing the rest. For that advantage we have been authorized to waive your charges."

The porcine face of the merchant brightened exponentially at this compliment, "Now that makes good business sense, sir. A good thing you came to me first, as there are others who do not share my vision."

"We were made aware of your reputation and your enthusiasm for our expansion of the telephone system in this area," replied Holmes. "That made you the man for us!"

135

"Well, well, that's fine, just fine!" he said again clasping his hands together. "Where do we start?"

Holmes smiled, explaining that we would go to his businesses to take pictures of the outside and inside of each. We would include employees and customers in poses of conducting business and then, allow him to choose those he wished for publication. He suggested emphatically that we start with the pharmacy shop, due to its photogenic atmosphere. If those pictures were deemed agreeable to O'Malley, we would move on to his other businesses in the near future.

O'Malley was all in agreement. We set 10:00 a.m. Friday for our first job.

Chapter Eighteen

We indulged in a hearty breakfast then gathered up the photography equipment and set off for the pharmacy shop.

"Mr. Scott, Mr. Wilson! Good morning to you, sirs!" boomed the voice of O'Malley as we arrived at his first business.

"I've explained what you are planning. Our pharmacist, Mr. Henshaw, and the assistant, Ryan, will help you as you please. Do you have any idea how long you will be?"

As we rehearsed it, I answered first. "The sunshine will do for the outside shots on a fine day like today," I replied. Then, stepping inside, I put on a bit of a frown and declared. "Hmm, this could be difficult. We'll have to catch the morning light coming through the windows quickly before the sun rises much farther overhead. We'd better shoot the indoor scenes first. That way, we'll also be out of your way before any lunch hour customers drop by."

"Splendid, splendid!" cried the businessman, clapping his meaty hands together.

"Well then, I'll be off and await your results."
Holmes thanked him and we unloaded our equipment. Holmes and I, with Ryan's help, re-arranged some displays so we could set the camera up for a well-lit angle of the counter. The clerk was the epitome of his Irish roots and,

were it not for his height of about five foot, nine inches, could have easily passed for a Leprechaun with his red hair, goatee and broad smile.

Henshaw, on the other hand, busied himself filling prescriptions, avoiding the manual tasks we set ourselves to. He was slightly shorter than Holmes, but broader of girth. His black hair had receded halfway back upon his crown. His mutton chop whiskers and handlebar moustache were beginning to grey corresponding with his age approaching fifty.

At last, we were in position with proper lighting and reflectors to reduce shadows and obtain clean, sharp pictures. While we had been setting up, a few customers had wandered in and Ryan waited on them. The latest person to do so was a charming woman of about twenty-two, simply attired in a dark red dress and a small black hat. Her hair was a chestnut brown and her eyes sparkled with youthful enthusiasm.

Holmes intruded into her shopping with his smoothest charm and explained what we were doing. He asked if she would mind posing as a customer for us.

Shyly she agreed and Holmes positioned her at the counter, standing at an angle that would give us a profile shot of her and of Henshaw as he handed her a prescription.

"If you please, Miss," he instructed, "will you put out your right hand about here?" He held her elbow and manoeuvred her hand into place.

"Now you, Mr. Henshaw, please pick up a box of pills, any will do, and act as though you were about to hand it to her. Oh, are you left-handed, Mr. Henshaw?"

"No, Mr. Scott," he answered, "I just thought that since my left hand is closer to her right hand it would be more convenient and would allow me to look toward the camera."

"Logical, sir," answered Holmes, hiding his disappointment. "But what we are trying to portray in this shot is your care for your customer." Holmes took the box from the druggist grip and placed it into his right hand. Doing so, he pulled up Henshaw's sleeve at the elbow to reduce wrinkles in his shirt and grasped his wrist to turn the box at an angle where the label could be seen.

"There, now look directly into her eyes. Smile, as if you were giving a present to your daughter."

A shadow passed across the man's face. "I have no daughter, sir," he said rather defensively.

Holmes replied, "Ah, you misunderstand me. You must look at this scene as a vignette in a play and you are one of the actors. As an actor you summon up your character by pretending to do or be something, even if it's not true."

Henshaw 'harrumphed' but managed a passable smile while his customer did the same. I took two pictures then Holmes then whispered to me, "One more, move the camera closer and focus on their hands."

"Hold still, please," I asked and moved the camera's tripod a few feet. "I want to get a close up of this transaction to show 'helping hands'."

Triggering off the next flash explosion I announced, "That will do, Miss, thank you very much. Now, Mr. Ryan, for a more formal shot I'd like you to stand next to Mr. Henshaw behind the counter ..."

We continued on this way for several more minutes, then moved outside the store. Once finished, we packed up our equipment and bid farewell to the shop staff.

As we drove back to the inn, Holmes instructed me on what he wanted done with the pictures after I returned to Mr. Bailey in London to have them developed. I naturally agreed to perform these functions.

"By the way," I ventured, "that seemed very sound acting advice you gave to Henshaw. Where did you pick that up?"

"I confess, I spent two of my university long vacations performing with Henry Irving and his troupe. Had my mind taken a different turn from its problem solving needs, I believe I would have made a fair actor."

"I always thought so, my friend." I replied.

We had not gone far while this conversation had taken place when suddenly, Holmes ordered the cab driver to stop and proceeded to bid me farewell.

"But, Scott," I cried (remembering in time to use his alias), "Will you not join me for lunch? Certainly we have much to discuss."

"Not now, Wilson. Our two mysterious gentlemen just passed us, wheeling their way toward the pharmacy. I intend to pursue that curiosity while the trail is warm. You'll have just time to enjoy your meal and catch the 3:30 train to London to reach Bailey's before closing. I'll be waiting for the photos with tomorrow's afternoon post."

He then hailed a cab going back the way we had come. I sighed and told the driver to press on. At the Inn I instructed the porter to store the trunk in the lobby, as I would be leaving on the afternoon train. Offering him a healthy tip, I proceeded to the restaurant where I was able to sample another of their fine luncheon selections before my return to that teeming mass of humanity that is London.

*　　*　　*

I arrived at Bailey's shop just a few minutes before 5:00 and returned his trunk with his equipment. I pointed out the plates I had used and gave him Holmes's instructions regarding the size he wanted the photos and how many to produce.

"Three sets, at eight inch by ten inch, you say?"

"Only of those with people in them. Two each of the others will be sufficient." I replied.

Bailey contemplated, "Well, that will take a bit of time. Best I work on it tonight so you can get them in the morning post in time for afternoon delivery to Holmes."

Arranging a time to retrieve the photos Holmes required, I then set off for home to find my sweet Mary waiting, with a roast in the oven and a lovely table set.

"Hello, my darling," she exclaimed as she hugged me warmly after I had hung my hat and coat. "I took a chance that Mr. Holmes would not keep you overnight and helped Ivy put up your favourite for dinner."

"Why, this is wonderful, my Love! What's the occasion?"

"The occasion being that my hospital stay and this case has kept us from an evening alone together far too long. After Ivy has cleared the dinner dishes I've given her the night off. Because, *Doctor*, I want you all to myself tonight!"
Uscita discretamente.

Chapter Nineteen

The next morning, over buttered muffins and coffee, Mary told me she had spent the previous afternoon visiting our client in the hospital.

"She received some more flowers," she offered, as she refilled my coffee.

"Not anonymously this time?" I queried, as she sat beside me.

"No, these were an arrangement of various coloured carnations from Mr. Salmon, with a card wishing her a speedy recovery and a promise to visit soon."

"They really should get together and draw up her will."

"So you think that may be the motive? Her stepfather, then, is a suspect?"

"He's certainly not beyond suspicion." I answered. "Although he is not left-handed. A surly fellow, though, and apparently preoccupied. Most likely caused by his financial straits."

"Lilly did have one other visitor," Mary continued "Besides Caroline, who is always there now, Mr. Ferguson came by, bearing a gift of chocolates."

"Well, that should do her no harm so long as she does not overindulge." I smiled.

"Yes, I think that relationship has possibilities. At least I hope so." Mary sighed and asked, "What time do you need to leave for Bailey's?"

"In a few minutes," I answered, snatching her hand as she reached to clear my dishes. "But first I need to thank you for a lovely evening."

We shared a lingering kiss, ultimately disrupted by the bell at the door. Answering it, I accepted a telegram and paid off the lad who delivered it.

"From Holmes, no doubt," stated Mary. "The man has a penchant for inconvenient interruptions," she smiled coquettishly.

"Yes, it's from Holmes." I replied, "He wishes me to bring the photographs back in person, as well as my medical bag. Apparently, he has need of my presence in pursuit of a lead."

Mary put her arms around my neck and transfixed me with her large blue eyes. "And you must go," she intoned. "Is there anything I can do?"

Giving her another kiss, I reminded her that her visits to Miss Fontaine were the best thing for the lady's recovery. The information about her visitors could prove illuminating, as well.

After re-packing my portmanteau, I shrugged into my coat and retrieved my hat and stick. Mary then entered the room, hands clasped behind her.

"You just be careful, John," she commanded. "And don't forget these!"

In her hands she held out my Webley revolver and an extra box of cartridges.

*　*　*

I was off again to Bailey's and picked up the photographs, then on to St. Pancras Station where I caught the last morning train. Shortly after noon I was again alighting, only this time there was no Holmes to greet me, as he was not aware which train I would be taking.

I caught a cab and arrived at the Glenlyn House, whereupon I was given the same room as previously. I unpacked my bag and began to open my door to step over to Holmes's room when his door opened. A man I had never seen was stepping out and locking the door behind him. He looked suspiciously up and down the hallway, apparently fearing to be observed. I held back momentarily with my door barely cracked open to observe him. He was an older gentleman, lean and one or two inches under six feet with a slightly bowed back. His hair was grey and curly. He had a full beard and moustache peppered with black and grey. He wore silver framed spectacles, a tweed suit with a dark brown bowler hat and carried an oak walking stick with a brass handle. His actions were all too suspicious for me and I stepped out into the hall to confront him.

"You, sir!" I exclaimed, as his back was to me. "What is your business there?"

He turned and fixed his gaze upon me. "What business is that of yours, sir?" he challenged in a low gravelly voice.

"That is my friend's room and your presence does not appear to be authorized," I snarled back.

"Your friend, you say?" he cocked an eyebrow. "You claim to know this Mr. William Scott?"

"We are business associates, yes."

"And what business would that be?"

Recalling our cover story I answered, "We are working on a telephone directory for this area."

"Really? I find that hard to believe," he sneered as he reached for his pocket.

"Stop right there!" I commanded as I pulled my Webley from my own pocket and pointed it at his chest.

A look of astonishment came across his features as he, no doubt, did not expect me to be armed. He looked up and down the hall as if to make sure we were alone and then lowered his voice.

"Watson, you really do surprise me!"

"Holmes?" I responded in a hoarse whisper as I peered closely to try to penetrate his disguise.

"Yes old friend. Quickly, let's step back inside and I'll bring you up to date."

I pocketed my revolver and we closeted ourselves back into my own hotel room.

Seated again across from each other, I enquired, "What is this disguise all about, Holmes?"

"You remember the two gentlemen who showed up, first at Henshaw's home just as I was leaving, and again when I left you yesterday? I found that they did indeed stop in at the pharmacy and took Henshaw to lunch."

"But what is their business with Henshaw?"

"That, good Doctor, I have not yet ascertained, but I hope to do so by the fact that I was able to retain this very room for you. You brought your medical bag, I see."

"As you asked, Holmes" I replied. "But what do you have in mind?"

"It will be of significant use to me, Watson. I have need of a certain instrument of yours. The bag itself will also allow me to complete another avenue that has opened."

He went on to explain his disguise was to ensure that the two strange men were not, in fact, following him. He would be making a call in this guise, using my bag to establish himself as a visiting physician at a local sanatorium.

"How does this sanatorium enter into the picture?" I asked.

"I do not know," he responded, "But I followed Henshaw yesterday after he closed shop. He stopped and stayed there for over an hour. I intend to infiltrate and see what can be learned."

Changing subjects, he disclosed that he had 'run into' Ryan as he left the apothecary shop upon Henshaw's return from lunch. He offered to treat the young man to a meal.

"Much can be gleaned over a friendly repast, Watson. Did you bring the photos?"

I pulled the packet out of my luggage and handed them over to Holmes. He flipped through them rapidly until he found one in particular.

"Aha!" he exclaimed, "This confirms my supposition. Do you see the lighter shade of skin tone on this upper portion of Henshaw's right wrist?"

I took the photo of the 'helping hands' that Holmes had insisted on me shooting. I examined it closely with the magnifying glass he had pulled from his pocket. There was, indeed, a marked difference in the shades of grey on the man's wrist.

"What does it mean, Holmes?" I asked, handing the photo and glass back to him.

"When I took Henshaw's hand to position it for this photograph, there was a perceptible tensing on his part. He was reacting as though an awkward movement might cause him pain. While I was initially disappointed at his not being left-handed, this reaction renewed my hopes that perhaps his right hand had been injured in some way, forcing him to use his left. The tan line you note here shows that his forearm was wrapped in bandages for some time. During my conversation with Ryan I ascertained that Henshaw had, indeed, injured his arm several weeks ago, though Ryan does not know how."

"That would explain the left-handed use of the wrench on the pipe," I posed.

"Indeed, Watson. As well as the reason why it slipped while he was using it awkwardly with an unfamiliar hand.

"I also confirmed that he was in London during the times of the falling curtain, the runaway horse and the leaking gas line. There is only one problem," he said, lighting a cigarette.

"What is that?"

Through the first puff of smoke he squint his eyes and declared, "He has not been back to the city for six weeks. There is no way he could have put the poison in Fontaine's milk."

* * *

We spent the next half hour going over plans for the day. I was to take one set of photos to Mr. O'Malley for his review. Holmes advised me to take another with me when I returned home. I was to show them around to livery stables and at the theatre to establish Henshaw's presence and possible involvement.

147

While I was gone, he took my bag and departed for the sanatorium in Barnet, a couple miles to the north. Posing as a visiting physician, he gleaned the information he was seeking. When I returned from O'Malley's, I found him in my room straightening out the rug, my medical bag on the bed. The false beard and wig were gone and he was dressed as himself again.

"Ah, Watson! Was our client pleased with the photographs?"

"Mr. O'Malley is more than satisfied, Holmes," I said shrugging out of my coat and hanging it up. "He is most eager to pursue this project with utmost haste. When this is all over how are we to explain that there is no such project? Will we just disappear and leave him holding on to false hopes?"

"A minor detail, Doctor. I will deal with it when this case is finished."

"And how did your day go?" I enquired. "Did you learn anything at the sanatorium?"

"Yes, Watson. I had revised my theory regarding Henshaw into thinking he had a confederate, possibly the missing wife. Unfortunately, I shall have to reconsider the facts."

"What happened?"

"Mrs. Henshaw is suffering from a nervous breakdown. She has been confined to the Barnet Sanatorium for three months."

I frowned, knowing that this information disrupted his theory. Hoping to draw out some better news, I asked about the two gentlemen who had been seen with Henshaw.

"I'm afraid I have fared no better there, Watson. Their business is totally unrelated to our case. If you will excuse me, my friend, I must retire to my room and ponder over a pipe or two. Feel free to dine without me. I believe we will be returning to London in the morning."

With no further explanation, he retired to his own room. I dashed off a telegram to Mary and settled down with a book until dinner-time.

Chapter Twenty

The next day being Sunday, our return home on the early morning train was quiet, as most travellers were still attending worship services. The peals of several church bells greeted our ears as we glided along the rails into London and arrived at St. Pancras. Holmes deigned not to speak during this journey, but sat quietly smoking his pipe and staring out the window; though I am sure he saw nothing but whatever was in his mind's eye.

Upon our arrival we parted. He returned to Baker Street and I to Mary, at home in Kensington. Each of us took a set of the photos. I was to check livery stables to see if anyone had rented a conveyance to Henshaw, while Holmes would return to the theatre to see if anyone recognized the pharmacist as being in or near the premises. He had decided not to completely abandon his theory that Henshaw had a confederate. However, he also told me that he was going to be returning his mind to an examination of all other suspects.

Arriving at home, I found Mary about to depart for St. Bartolomew's. She delayed her departure long enough for me to take a quick lunch, whereupon I told her of Holmes discoveries. We then engaged a cab and wound our way through the busy Sunday afternoon streets to arrive at the hospital about 2:00.

Entering Miss Fields' room however, was not the happy

occasion I would have expected. Upon our opening of the door we found, instead of the recuperating actress, an empty made up bed and no sign of occupancy.

* * *

Holmes, meanwhile, had resumed his investigation at the Lyceum, armed with the photos of Henshaw. He questioned several performers and stage crew regarding the man with little result. Some thought he looked familiar, but could not be sure. Figgins was pre-occupied with the upcoming matinee, but the cursory glance that he afforded the photo was inconclusive.

Only Washburn, the stage door guardian, held out any hope for Holmes. He was fairly certain that he had seen the man back around the time the gasmen were making their installation. He had assumed he was one of the crew.

"Of course, he weren't dressed like that, Mr. Holmes," stated the big man, pointing to the picture. "He wore overalls like most of the other workers. Only reason I noticed him at all was that he always held his arm half bent. Like it should have been in a sling. Seemed to be an awkward way to work if you ask me, but I thought maybe he had an old war wound or something, so I didn't question it."

Holmes thanked him and pondered his next move over a smoke. The matinee had started by this time, so there was little opportunity for further questioning. He crushed out his cigarette and with a purposeful stride, exited the theatre and hailed a cab for Scotland Yard.

* * *

Finding no sign of Miss Fields in her room Mary and I immediately sought out information at the nurse's station. We were informed that she had left the hospital in the company of a man that morning. 'Some theatre fellow who had been here before'. The gentleman seemed in a hurry and she had not left a note. The nurse assumed she was going home as Dr. Kennedy had cleared her for release.

Armed with this information we set out for the actress's apartment. We speculated on who this 'theatre fellow' might be, hoping that it was Ferguson, but concerned that it might have been Colby, since his new-found attitude had not yet been proven. Arriving there about 2:30, we hurried up the stairs and found no answer to the ringing of the bell or persistent knocking with the knob of my cane. Our questioning of the landlord revealed only that he noticed young Caroline leaving with a man and a large suitcase early that morning. He had seen no one come in or out since.

We now decided the theatre was our next destination. We could report to Holmes and confront Ferguson, in hopes of discovering our client's whereabouts.

*   *   *

Holmes, however, had long since left for the Yard. Upon his arrival he enquired after Lestrade and was informed that the Inspector was not working that Sunday. Recalling my report of Mary's interview with Dryden, he then asked to see Detective Brooke.

Having neglected to describe the young woman to Holmes, I now offer her description, as noted by the author of her later adventures as a private detective by her Boswell, Catherine Louisa Pirkis: She was not tall, she was not short; she was not dark, she was not fair; she was neither handsome nor ugly. Her features were altogether nondescript; her one noticeable trait was a habit she had, when absorbed in thought, of dropping her eyelids over her eyes till only a line of eyeball showed, and she appeared to be looking out at the world through a slit, instead of through a window.

Holmes explained to Miss Brooke that he wished to speak with Dryden regarding the case in hand.

Looking him up and down she responded, "I see you've had a very busy day, Mr. Holmes. A morning train trip and a visit to the Lyceum, I believe. As your friend, Dr. Watson, might say, I prescribe a few moments rest, so I will bargain with you, sir. A visit to Mr. Dryden, in exchange for a half hour of your time afterward, over a cup of coffee at The Riverbank Restaurant down the street."

Holmes peered at the young woman with a new appreciation. He replied in turn, "Provided I do not glean any information requiring immediate action, then I shall be at your disposal Miss Brooke. Shall we go?"

Upon their entering Dryden's cell the actor again stood and offered the lady his only chair.

"And who is this, Miss Brooke?" he enquired with a sardonic smile "Another prosecutor from the court? Don't tell me they have you fellows working the Sabbath now?"

Holmes drew himself to his full height and stared down at the shorter man. "I am Sherlock Holmes, Mr. Dryden. No doubt you will recall that I am seeking the truth in the Lorraine Fontaine case. A truth that will either free you, or condemn you. Now, if you will sit down I have some further questions."

The comedian lost his smile and sat on the bed, but without complete surrender to Holmes's presence he stated, "Then I will be a free man, Mr. Holmes, for I have had no part in any untoward action toward Miss Fontaine."

Holmes digested that statement for a moment, then pulled the photos from his inner coat pocket and handed them to Dryden.

"I need you to look over these photographs carefully, Mr. Dryden. Tell me if you see anyone you recognize, keeping in mind that they may have been dressed quite differently when you saw them."

Slowly, the actor went through the photos. He paused briefly when he came to the one of Henshaw and Ryan posed formally behind the counter. He shook his head and kept on. Again he paused and studied the photo of Henshaw and his female customer very closely.

After he finished going through them all, he handed them back to Holmes with a question. "How old are these photographs, Mr. Holmes?"

"They were taken last week, why?"

"I thought I recognized the girl as one of Colby's actresses. I worked for him briefly four years ago. She should be much older than the girl in that picture though. How old is she?"

"Approximately twenty-two," answered Holmes.

"No, the woman I'm thinking of would be at least thirty by now."

"You also paused at the picture of the two gentlemen. Did you recognize one of those men?"

"I thought so, at first," replied Dryden "but the man I'm thinking of I only saw briefly by the back door of the theatre. It's hard to be certain with these black and white photographs."

"When was that?" asked Holmes.

"About three, maybe four, weeks ago," the actor recalled. "I'm not sure, but this fellow here may have been the man I saw at the stage door handing a package to Washburn." He pointed at the photograph and Holmes repressed a smile. Dryden's finger was not on Henshaw, but on the Irish clerk, Ryan. "If his hair is red I remember thinking that he looked like a tall Leprechaun."

*   *   *

Upon our arrival at the Lyceum, Mary and I discovered the matinee well under way and learned that Holmes had left some time before. Our only choice was to wait for intermission so that we could speak with Ferguson.

The acts seemed to drag on intolerably. At last the curtain rang down for the interval and we were able to corner the director for interrogation.

"I am sorry, Mrs. Watson, Doctor," he replied to our inquest, "We left a note to be delivered to Constable MacDonald only. I should have sent word to you, as well. Loraine was getting restless, confined to that hospital room. Dr. Kennedy said she could be released, provided she did not attempt to go back to work for at least two more weeks and checked in with him at the slightest sign of discomfort or recurring symptoms. I still fear for her safety, so Caroline and I bundled her off in secret to Hazlitt's Hotel in Soho Square.

We checked her in as my sister under the name 'Lilly Ferguson' to maintain her anonymity. I left a private note to be given to the policeman so he can continue his protection rounds in Soho. I also dispatched young Drew to keep an eye out for any suspicious characters hanging about. I assure you, she should be quite safe."

This was welcome news, indeed. We left Ferguson to continue with his matinee and departed. We decided to drop in on Holmes to inform him of this turn of events, then to go on to Soho to pay Mary's friend a visit.

* * *

Holmes, having obtained this new information from Dryden regarding the possibility of Ryan being a courier, kept up his end of the bargain with Miss Brooke and sat with her in a booth at the the Riverbank Restaurant.

"You are quite observant, Miss Brooke," he began after the waiter had taken their order. "Would you care to explain your conclusions about my day's activities?"

The woman smiled as she folded her strong hands on the table between them. "I've always prided myself on an eye for detail, Mr. Holmes. Your railway journey was evident by the ticket stub protruding from your waistcoat pocket. There is also a smudge of greasepaint on your left elbow. As you are an otherwise very fastidious dresser, according to Dr. Watson's writings, I took it that this was a fresh stain obtained by a visit to a theatre or a theatrical shop. The trip to the Lyceum, I admit, was an assumption since that is the theatre at which this case is so involved."

"Bravo, Miss Brooke!" Holmes exclaimed as their coffee arrived. "Now what is it you wish to discuss with me that takes us both from our duties?"

Shifting in her seat slightly, the young lady launched into her request. "I've heard talk of your work from several of my colleagues, Mr. Holmes. Mostly praiseworthy, although I'll admit there is some professional jealousy among the ranks at the Yard. Lestrade is grudgingly impressed by your results, if not your methods. Hopkins wishes he could have you on

154

every case. I've read both of Dr. Watson's published works and after all that, I see you as a great source of the science of detection."

"How you could have gained that from Watson's romanticizing of my work shows a perception that will serve you well," answered Holmes. "He so often omits or glosses over the science of the work. What should have been textbook examples are reduced to gimmickry of near fictional proportions."

"As I suspected, Mr. Holmes," continued the woman. "You must be aware it is difficult for a woman to make her way in the man's world of police work.

The prejudice is such that I have been considering leaving the force as I've had overtures from a private agency."

Holmes gave her a sincere look and said "That would be a pity for Scotland Yard, Miss Brooke. But, I certainly understand your position. Frankly, I could never have worked under the constraints or the narrow thinking of the official police force. How can I help you?"

Leaning forward so that her chin was only inches above her folded hands, she stared at Holmes with determined eyes and stated her case, "I want to learn from you, Mr. Holmes. I want the freedom to call upon you to assist me in my cases when you are available. I want to read whatever monographs you have produced in the science of detection and the art of deduction. I want to be able to sit with you from time to time like this and discuss how to observe and how to string together facts and events into hypotheses. To learn how to prove those hypotheses. in order to solve cases and bring about justice."

Holmes took a long slow draught of his coffee and set his cup down with a studied eye upon the female detective. Her best poker face could not hide her anxiety at waiting for his answer.

"My dear Miss Brooke," he at last pronounced. "I would be happy to assist you all that I can. Far be it from me to deny my knowledge to someone who genuinely wants to learn.

Feel free to call upon me at any time and, if convenient, I shall be happy to impart whatever wisdom I can to you."

She bowed her head in gratitude and looked back up with a smile, "Thank you, Mr. Holmes."

"In fact," he replied, "let us begin right now while we finish our coffee. Tell me what you observed about our waiter, before he returns."

With the gauntlet thus thrown, Brooke took up the challenge.

"He is approximately five feet eight inches tall and eleven stone in weight. Age about twenty. Dark complexion, clean-shaven, brown eyes, black hair parted on the left side and of medium length. He speaks with a slight accent that appears to be Italian, but he has been in this country long enough that it is barely noticeable. He is right handed, and married just recently."

"Excellent, Miss Brooke!" answered her newly designated mentor. "You have superb powers of observation. Now, let me add just some minor details for you. He *is* of Italian descent, but is either first born generation English or came here as an infant. The accent you noticed is that of one who has lived under the roof of Italian parents, while not being his native tongue. His recent marriage is evident by his occasional twirling of his wedding ring, which he is not yet used to, as you observed. He came to this job just recently and was required to shave his moustache by the rules of this establishment, as his upper lip is still slightly paler than his face. He is near the end of his shift, evidenced by an egg yolk stain on his left sleeve obtained during breakfast servings this morning and the working up of his shirttail, as it is nearly un-tucked through his exertions of the day."

*   *   *

While Holmes was thus engaged, Mary and I dropped in upon Mrs. Hudson, who embraced my wife with sisterly affection and informed us that Holmes was out. I ascended the seventeen steps to our old quarters and left him a note of explanation while Mary enjoyed a quick cup of tea with my former landlady. Upon my return to the ladies, I declined tea for myself, but only with the promise that we would be back soon for a longer visit.

Mary and I then engaged a cab for the drive to Soho Square and the Hazlitt Hotel. This establishment is actually housed in three historic buildings in Soho Square, and is considered one of London's best small hotels. Built in 1718, the hotel is named after William Hazlitt, who founded the Unitarian Church in Boston and wrote four volumes on the life of his hero, Napoleon.

Hazlitt's is a favourite with artists, actors and models, which explained its attraction for Lionel Ferguson. It's eclectic and filled with odds and ends picked up around the country at estate auctions. Some find its Georgian decor a bit Spartan, but the many original prints hanging on the walls brighten it considerably. Some of the floors dip and sway, but that is all part of the charm.

Upon our arrival, we were greeted out front by young Drew who promptly escorted us to Miss Fontaine's room. She and Caroline were reading and sewing respectively. Miss Fontaine's health was much improved and, except for tiring easily, she appeared eager to return to the stage.

After a thoroughly enjoyable visit, Mary and I returned home for a quiet dinner and relaxing evening. Having no further word from Holmes, I resolved to make the rounds of livery stables the next day to ascertain if Henshaw could be proven to be in London on the day Miss Fontaine was nearly run down.

Chapter Twenty-One

Whilst I was showing Henshaw's photograph around various carriage houses and livery stables, Holmes was continuing his investigations into the possible suspects. He also engaged in correspondence with Miss Brooke by sending her some of his various monographs in relation to the arts of criminal science, observations and deductions.

One of his excursions on Tuesday led him to drop in on our client at Hazlitt's where he was intercepted by the ever-alert young Drew and shown to Miss Fontaine's room. While there, he showed the photographs of Henshaw to the actress, her servant and the lad. None claimed to recognize him, but admitted that, as crowded as the theatre was with its various acts, stagehands and labourers, it was hard to say.

That morning, Holmes sent a message to Miss Brooke, calling attention to one of the monographs he had sent her and suggesting that she also call on Miss Fontaine to further question her on the possibility of rejected suitors or other envious persons such as Miss Harley. He also dashed off a telegram to the local constabulary in Woodside Park to, as he put it, "follow another thread which could tie things up nicely".

Meanwhile, I had found a livery stable near St. Pancras station where one of the grooms thought he recognized Henshaw. It had been some time ago, but he was able to check the date, as there had been some damage to the wagon. It was circumstantial evidence and I duly reported it to Holmes.

Another disturbing event occurred on Thursday when I was stopped by Hazlitt's and found young Drew confronting none other than Harrison Colby out front.

My wife's description of him left no doubt as to the identity of this little man with the dark hair slicked back under his top hat, waxed moustache worn in handlebar fashion and dressed in his dark clothing. He appeared more of a magician en route to his performance than a man about town running errands on a spring day.

The boy was standing between Colby and the hotel entrance asking him his business. Such impertinence made Colby impatient and I could see him physically tense. I hurried my pace forward before any further confrontation ensued.

"Harrison Colby?" I enquired and he turned at this new intrusion upon his mission.

Giving Drew a warning look and stepping between them, I faced the man and asked again, "Aren't you Harrison Colby, the theatrical producer?"

Turning and giving me an inquisitive look he answered. "I am sir, and who might you be?"

"Dr. John Watson, at your service. What brings you this way today?"

"I am here to call upon Miss Loraine Fontaine. I understand she has taken rooms here at the Hazlitt."

"Is she expecting you, then?" I replied.

"I told her I would be keeping in touch when last I saw her. What business would that be of yours?" he asked, eyeing me narrowly.

"As her physician," I answered, stretching the truth a bit. "I am overseeing her care while she convalesces. As such, I have advised her to limit her visitors as much as possible so she can rest and regain her strength. How did you discover that she was here and not returned to her apartment?"

His face softened somewhat. "I see. I was unaware that her condition was still so delicate. Some of my own performers are staying here and she is too recognizable to remain incognito for long. If you would please, just tell her that I called to express my well wishes and I hope she will rejoin her troupe soon." He handed me his card and went on his way.

"I don't trust that man, Doctor," Drew exclaimed. "He's got a bad look about 'im."

"I understand, Drew. Mr. Colby's reputation is certainly not sterling. However, I'm told that he has expressed a change in his life that will make him and his productions more amenable to the theatre-going public. I believe we should reserve judgment until that proves itself one way or the other."

"Hmpf, I'll still keep an eye on 'im," declared the lad.

"You do that, son. In the meantime I think I'll drop in and see Miss Fontaine."

"Oh there's a Scotland Yard lady in there now. I showed her in just a few minutes ago."

"Ah, that must be Miss Brooke. I'll just pop in for a quick hello, then."

The boy followed me through the hotel to Miss Fontaine's rooms and just as we arrived, the door was opened by the young lady.

"Miss Brooke, a pleasure to see you," I said, doffing my hat. She nodded her head and put out her hand to shake mine. The delicate fingers enfolding mine were feminine, yet strong. "Doctor, I am very pleased to see you as well."

She stepped back into the room and I greeted our client who was sitting in a wingback chair sipping tea.

"Good afternoon, Miss Fontaine. I just thought I'd drop in and see how you were feeling."

"I am extremely well, Doctor, thank you. Although I am suffocating being cooped up in these rooms. I feel a need for exercise. A walk about the square in the sunshine would be most welcome."

"I'm not sure that would be wise, "I replied. "It is already known that you are here. Some actor or another reported your presence to Harrison Colby. I just intercepted him outside and told him you were not up to visitors yet." I handed her his card.

"We were just discussing Mr. Colby, among others," interjected Miss Brooke. "Fortunately the hotel has a security man and Constable MacDonald is patrolling the area at night. Still it may be wise to move you again to a more discreet location," she added, nodding at our client.

"Somewhere out in the country, I hope," replied the actress, with some exasperation.

"Well, I would imagine we should discuss that with Mr. Holmes. What do you think, Doctor?" the Miss Brooke asked, gazing at me.

"Quite right," I answered.

Miss Fontaine lowered her head to her teacup in resignation then suddenly looked back up at me. "Where are my manners? Doctor, would you like some tea?"

Grateful for a change of subject, I accepted and sat in a chair opposite the lady while she called for Caroline to bring in some more tea.

Miss Brooke chose this moment to excuse herself, "I shall be off to the Yard then."

Turning to the young stagehand she said, "And you will be going back on duty as well, I suppose?"

The boy drew himself up to his full, if diminutive, height and replied "Yes, ma'am, no one will get in here without my knowin' it!"

She smoothed back young Drew's hair behind his ear and cupped his chin in her hand. "You're doing an excellent job, young man. Keep up the good work."

The lad beamed with a mixture of pride and embarrassment and he walked out with her, while I finished my tea with the actress.

* * *

162

I chose to drop in on Holmes once more before proceeding home to dinner. I reported the appearance of Colby at the Hazlitt and enquired as to whether we should remove Miss Fontaine to a more remote location. His answer surprised me.

"No, Watson, that won't be necessary. Our client is no longer in immediate danger."

"You've solved the case, then?" I responded in surprise.

"I am awaiting confirmation from the telegrams I sent earlier, but yes, I believe our threads have presented a rather intriguing tapestry that is now complete."

"Does this have anything to do with those gentlemen who seemed to be following you?" I asked.

"What?" he asked, rather distractedly as he attempted to light his pipe. "Oh, no they are not involved at all."

"You've discovered their identity?"

"Oh yes, thanks to you. While you were engaged with Mr. O'Malley, I returned to your room in time to use your stethoscope and eavesdrop upon our mysterious strangers in the room below. They are investors seeking to purchase a specific group of estates in the area so as to construct the North Middlesex Golf Club. I realize some golfers are passionate about their sport, but I do not believe murder was on the minds of these men."

"Then who is the culprit, Holmes?"

"All in good time, Watson. I'd rather not commit myself until the last thread is tied. I should receive my answers tonight, or tomorrow at the latest, and all will be revealed."

Thus, I bid Holmes a good night and returned home to enjoy a quiet dinner with Mary.

Chapter Twenty-Two

Apparently, Holmes received his answers early the following morning. I found myself invited to his rooms for tea on that Friday afternoon, with a request that Mary drop in on Miss Fontaine at that same hour.

Arriving shortly before four o'clock, I was just in time to follow Mrs. Hudson up the stairs with her tea service. I greeted my friend, who sat smoking a cigar and reading an afternoon paper.

"Come in, Watson! Thank you, Mrs. Hudson," he cried. "Take a seat, old friend, and enjoy a cigar, courtesy of Mr. Irving."

I settled into my old chair and lit one of the cigars proffered by Holmes. It was an excellent smoke, with a delightful vanilla flavour.

As we smoked and drank tea in the sitting room at Baker Street, I confess that the many aspects of this case had left my mind spinning with the possibilities and multiple suspects that had arisen.

Suddenly, Holmes made a pronouncement that the culprit would be arriving imminently and our case would be wrapped up.

This only heightened my curiosity as to how he had unravelled the truth amidst the tangled threads that had presented themselves.

"Holmes" I asked, "if we are expecting a cold-blooded killer to arrive, I should tell you that I do not have my revolver with me."

"No need, Watson," he replied. "I am sure there will be no violence here tonight. Ah, I believe our quarry is ascending the steps now."

At the door's knock, I stepped 'round to open it with some apprehension, not knowing who or what to expect. Instead of a fiendish criminal, however, I found myself looking down into the eager eyes of young Drew.

Turning to Holmes I said, "Apparently not yet." Then looking back to Drew I questioned him, "Have you something to report, Drew? We are expecting visitors momentarily."

Drew looked up at me and then to Holmes and answered, "No, sir, Dr. Watson. I'm 'ere at Mr. 'Olmes request."

Dumbfounded, I looked to my friend and his knowing smile betrayed his joy at my surprise.

"Come in, my boy," he intoned. "Take a seat and have some tea and cakes, if you like."

Without hesitation, the lad crossed the room and sat down, reaching for Mrs. Hudson's delicious cakes. I slowly closed the door and returned to my chair.

"What is the meaning of this, Holmes? Surely Drew is not the visitor you were describing to me just now?"

"A moment, please, Watson. All will become clear soon enough. Now," he said, turning again to our young guest, "I have some questions for you, young man. I can assure you that if you answer me truthfully, no harm will come of it and you will serve a far greater good."

"Anything you say, Mr. 'Olmes," he mumbled around a mouthful of cake.

"First of all, I would like you to tell Dr. Watson your full name."

The boy stopped, just as he was about to take another bite of cake, and looked at Holmes with what I can only describe as fear and panic. Sensing this, Holmes spoke quietly again.

"Trust me. Your father can no longer harm you. He is in the custody of Scotland Yard even as we speak.

"The Bobbies got 'im? What'd he do?"

Holmes gave me a quick glance and turned back to the boy. "He was caught stealing from his employer," he stated. "The point is, you are safe from him. Now please, tell Dr. Watson your name."

The lad turned to me with his eyes somewhat downcast and murmured, "Andrew Henshaw."

I confess that this news caused the cigar to slip from my fingers and I rushed to retrieve it from doing any damage to Mrs. Hudson's carpet.

"That's incredible!" I cried, stamping out the fallen ashes to ensure no sparks remained.

"It's very credible, Watson. In fact it's the thread that ties up our case. Andrew, if I may use your proper name, I need you to tell us about how you came to work at the theatre and about the powder your father told you to put in Miss Fontaine's milk."

"How'd you know I put the powder in her milk? Anyway it's *Drew*, if you please, sir. I never liked 'Andrew' 'cause that's what my father calls me. Fact is, I ran away from home a couple years ago. Made my way to London and was livin' here and there when I sees this poster out in front of the Lyceum with a lady's picture on it. She looked a lot like a picture my mother had up in the attic at home. Just a bit older. I wasn't ever supposed to go up in the attic, but there was lots o' stuff up there that was fun to play with, so I'd sneak up and found pictures and other things that belonged to a girl. But I didn't know who she was.

I couldn't ask my parents, since they'd know I'd gone in the attic, so I asked the maid and she said I must never ask about the girl, but that it was someone who used to live with us and went away shortly after I was born.

So, when I sees the picture at the theatre, I started hangin' around there and Mr. Figgy gave me a job running errands and cleaning up and all sorts of odds and ends. That's when I got to know Miss Fontaine. She's a real nice lady and a great actress."

"Yes, yes, An ... that is Drew," said Holmes, verging on impatience, but taking Drew's youth into consideration. "We are all very fond of Miss Fontaine. But tell us how it happened that your father convinced you to put the powder in her milk."

"Well sir, I was walkin' to the theatre one day and was just passing the front entrance, when this hand clamps down on my shoulder and another grabs my arm and wouldn't you know it, it's my old man.

"I tries to fight him off, tellin' him to leave me alone and I got a job and he ain't never gonna beat me again, 'cause I ain't ever comin' back, and he asks me where I was workin' and I pointed to the theatre.

"Well, the oddest look came over his face and he dragged me over to where Miss Fontaine's picture was and pointed at it and says to me, 'So you work here, do you, Andrew? Tell me everything you know about this woman.'

"So, I tell him that she's the star of the show and that she's a real nice lady and treats me real good. Then he asks me what she calls me, which I thought was a strange question so I tells him, 'Drew, just like everybody else since I left home.' Well, he got real quiet and thoughtful-like which scared me a little, but then he asked, 'Does anyone know your last name?' and I tells him 'no' 'cause I don't want his last name so I don't use one at all.

"'Well, that's fine, boy', he says 'if that's the way you want it. Since you're so determined to make it on your own, I'm going to help you get started ...'

Young Drew's narrative continued with Holmes asking questions along the way. We discovered that Henshaw made Drew sneak him into the theatre from time to time and he was present the day the curtain fell, but Drew said he was always careful not to let Miss Fontaine see him.

"Did your father ever show up at the theatre in workmen's clothes, or wearing anything with pockets large enough to conceal a pipe wrench?" queried Holmes "Especially around the time the gas men were working on the new pipes?"

"Oh yes, Mr. 'Olmes," the boy replied. "Especially then, 'cause he could hang about a bit more without anybody asking why he was there."

"On any of those occasions, did he leave you alone for awhile, say ten or fifteen minutes?"

"Sure he would. Sometimes he'd have to go off to the cloakroom or he'd say he wanted a look from a different angle and would leave me alone for a bit."

"And it was sometime after the gas leak in Miss Fontaine's dressing room that he began giving you the powder for her milk."

"Yes, sir. He said that she was a fine actress and could tell how much I liked her and so after the gas left her feeling so sickly, he gave me the powder and said to put a little in her milk pitcher every day and it would help her feel better. But that I shouldn't tell her 'cause actresses don't like other people taking credit for helping them."

Holmes looked at me and nodded toward the boy, "I believe that makes our case secure, Watson. Would you be so kind as to take young Drew here down to Mrs. Hudson's kitchen and ask her to make up a meal for him, for I perceive that these tea cakes are not about to satisfy the appetite of our adolescent friend."

Turning to our visitor he said, "You could use a proper meal couldn't you, Drew? I don't believe you've eaten since your eggs at breakfast."

"Aye sir. Too busy for lunch today."

"Very well, you go with Dr. Watson. We have some other visitors coming and I'll talk to you again afterwards."

I escorted Drew downstairs and put him in Mrs. Hudson's capable charge. Returning to our rooms I questioned Holmes. "I noted the dried egg yolk on his cheek as you must have, Holmes, but how did you conclude that he is an adolescent? I've assumed all along that he was about ten."

"You were judging him by his stature my friend. There are other signs of his pubescent onset. The occasional break of his voice, a tendency to scratch areas where new hairs are coming in, some acne, dandruff and other signs of hormonal changes."

"I get your point, Holmes," I interrupted. "What led you to believe that he was, in fact, Miss Fontaine's half-brother?"

"Ah that was a gift from his mother, for both he and Miss Fontaine have inherited specific physical characteristics that link their bloodline to her, especially about the ears and nose. There was enough resemblance to encourage my investigation along that path. I recalled that I had spotted no sign of a child inhabiting the Henshaw house. Yet she had told us of his birth. My answer was confirmed when I received a reply to the telegram I sent yesterday that stated Andrew Henshaw had not attended school in Woodside for two years and the constable's last report was that he had run away from home."

"Will his word stand up in court against his father?"

"Not to worry there, Watson. Lestrade found the poison used when he arrested Henshaw this morning. He, in fact, stole the chemicals from the pharmacy shop, so there won't be any trouble tracing it back to him as the only possible source. It was a concoction he made up himself, which was why we couldn't identify it."

"So, Henshaw was responsible from the beginning? The curtain, the wagon, the gas and the poisoned milk?"

"Actually, Watson, I believe the curtain was an accident. Witnessing that inspired Henshaw to the rest. When you found a livery where a man answering his description rented a wagon for the afternoon that our client was almost run down, it tied up that thread. All that was left was to ascertain how he could poison the milk when he wasn't in town. Once I observed Drew's family resemblance the answer presented itself. The poison, of course, was ingenious. By concocting his own from his pharmaceutical stock, he could make it as strong or diluted as he wished. Sending it to the theatre by way of Ryan kept him out of town and less likely to be suspect, and Ryan was unaware of the package contents. Eventually, Henshaw could let the poison build up in Miss Fontaine's system to the point of nearly untraceable death."

"Monstrous!" I declared. "That he should attempt to murder his wife's daughter and use his own son to commit the deed. I assume this was all due to Mr. Fields' original will and the assignment of property rights?"

"Yes, Watson, and Henshaw's time was running out. With his wife ill and possibly facing her own demise, he needed to eliminate Miss Fontaine. The estate would pass to her mother and then to him at her death. Should her mother die first, Fontaine's death, without a will of her own in place, as you discovered, would have the holdings split amongst several cousins, leaving Henshaw completely out of the picture. Of course this was all before our gentlemen from the North Middlesex Golf Club came upon the scene. Had they come but a few months ago with their offer to purchase the estate, none of this would have likely occurred."

"But why did not Miss Fields spot Henshaw lurking about the theatre?"

"I am sure, my friend, that he never allowed himself to be in close proximity to our client, and from a distance she would not be likely to recognize him. The years have not been kind to the man, for he has changed significantly since she lived at home. While I was there, I noted that his wedding picture shows him to be lean, clean-shaven and with a full head of hair. Since then he has gained forty pounds, his hair has receded, and he now has the mutton chop side whiskers and a handlebar moustache which we witnessed."

Holmes was standing and looking out the window to Baker Street below.

"Now, Watson, we have a delicate task. Miss Brooke has brought your wife and Miss Fontaine in response to my invitation. Do we tell our client of Drew's true identity? Do we mention his involvement in her poisoning? Or do we merely tell her that her father was responsible and is apprehended? What say you, good Doctor?"

Standing on my own I put out my cigar and said to Holmes, "I may be a 'good doctor', and I recall a foolish boast I once made of an experience of women over many nations and on three separate continents, but when it comes to the psychology of the female mind, marriage has opened my eyes and I consider myself an amateur, as any intelligent man should. Therefore, my good Holmes," I said, striding toward the door, "I shall intercept your guests and bring Mary up to answer your questions while I encourage Miss Fontaine and the Detective to enjoy the company of young Drew and Mrs. Hudson." Before he could respond, I was out the door and descending the steps to greet my wife and her friend.

* * *

Embracing Mary and greeting Miss Fontaine and Miss Brooke, I explained that Holmes was not quite ready for this consultation as yet. I informed the ladies that he needed to speak with Mary first. Mrs. Hudson, ever reliable, showed Miss Fontaine and Miss Brooke to her own sitting room where Drew was 'pleased as punch' to greet his favorite actress.

As I escorted Mary up the stairs, I briefly told her that Holmes had solved the case. However, he needed an opinion on how much he should reveal to his client. I thought she would know better than I, after all the recent time spent with her friend.

Entering Holmes sitting room again he bade Mary and me to sit.

"Mrs. Watson," he began, "first of all I must thank you for bringing me this case. It has been a most delightful exercise."

"You are quite welcome, Mr. Holmes. Thank you for solving it and putting Lilly out of harm's way. The culprit is apprehended?"

"Indeed, but as Watson must have told you, I desire an opinion as to how much detail I should reveal to Miss Fontaine. If you would favour me with an opinion as I lay out the facts before you.

"In return for the favour of my opinion I have one more small favour to ask of you, Mr. Holmes," my wife replied. I had no inkling as to what this might be.

"I'll certainly do what I can," he answered.

"We've known each other over two years now. You were best man at our wedding. You've been to our home on numerous occasions. Dragged my husband off on cases more times than I can remember. Would you *please* call me 'Mary'?"

Both Holmes and I were taken aback. Then he chuckled, "With your husband's permission, I would be honoured, *Mary*. If you will be so kind to address me as 'Holmes', without the 'Mister'."

They both looked to me and I merely stammered back, "I've certainly no objection if that's what you would like, Mary. But whatever made you think of that?"

"It just seems so awkward, John. You and he calling each other by your familiar names without titles attached. I think I've earned the right to be included in that familiarity."

"You have indeed!" cried Holmes. Then turning to me he said, "Do you see what I mean about the female mind, Watson? All this time I have addressed her with the title she so fittingly deserves as your wife, thinking I was being mindful of my manners, and yet she prefers the familiar."

"Well, old man," I replied, "you must admit that she is far more than just 'Mrs. Watson'. She has always been an intelligent woman in her own right. You have pointed this out on numerous occasions," as I smiled and reached out for her hand.

"Thank you, John," she smiled back and gave my hand a squeeze. "Now, *Holmes*, what can I do for you?"

Holmes explained the scenario and the fact that young Drew was actually the actresses' half-brother. He assured her that Drew knew nothing of the powder being poison and actually thought he was helping his idol.

"I see. Well, if it is my opinion you seek then I must tell you that you should tell Lilly everything. She is a grown woman and certainly mature enough to handle the truth. However," she looked sternly at each of us, "Drew must *not* be told that he was poisoning his sister. He is far too young to have to deal with the guilt of that, however misplaced."

"Should we be the ones to tell him that he is Lilly's half-brother?" I asked.

"I would leave that to Lilly, to tell him in her own time. But she must be aware of everything."

"Very well," said Holmes, standing. "Mary, I bow to your judgment in this instance. Watson, would you be good enough to escort Miss Fontaine up from Mrs. Hudson's company?"

*　*　*

As Miss Brooke remained with Drew, Holmes laid out the facts to our client. She was enraged at the thought of her step-father's fiendishness and quite taken aback by the revelation of her half-brother's identity.

"How could that beast use a child like that? It's totally unforgiveable! I hope he rots in prison."

"Attempted murder shall certainly put him away for a good long time, Miss Fontaine," said Holmes. "From the evidence gathered, his trial should be a mere formality. For all intents and purposes the case is closed."

"Closed?" queried Mary. "Hardly that, Holmes."

"Whatever do you mean, Mary?" I asked. "The man is arrested. He'll stand trial and go to jail for a very long time. What more is there?"

"John, you surprise me," she answered. "The criminal is apprehended and Lilly is free from fear. Yet, she still must recover her strength to continue her career. There are decisions to be made about young Drew. A will should obviously be written to eliminate such a motive in the future. And what of her mother?"

"My mother?" questioned the actress.

Mary took Lilly's hands in her own and looked her squarely in the eye. "Yes, Lillian, your mother. The woman is near death. Her son is too young to help. Her husband, demon that he is, at least provided for her. If she chooses, she can sell the estate to the golfers, but that still leaves her alone and ill."

Miss Fontaine pulled her hands from Mary's and looked away. "She turned her back on me when I needed her most. Apparently she did the same to Andrew, since he found it necessary to run away from home. She took that cad's word against mine, her own flesh and blood. She desecrated the memory of my father by not even giving him a decent mourning period." At this point she let go a sob and Mary placed an arm around her.

"Yes, Lilly, I know," she said quietly, holding her friend and rocking slowly. "All that she's done is hard to forgive. She was young and devastated at the loss of your father. This sweet talking charlatan came along and gave her comfort and a pretence of love. It blinded her to the truth because she was so desperately alone."

She turned Lilly to face her again. "You've never allowed yourself to love, Lilly. You don't know how wonderful and frightening it can be. The joys and the jealousies. The feelings that can override our better judgments. You cannot hold your mother responsible for all that when she was so vulnerable. You must at least go and see her. Extend the olive branch. Give her a chance."

At that point, Lilly fell sobbing into Mary's arms. I motioned to Holmes and we discreetly left them and descended upon Mrs. Hudson's parlour. We lit our cigars and engaged Drew and Miss Brooke in conversation.

Several minutes later Mary and her friend came downstairs, Lilly's tears gone, but eyes still a bit red. The ever-observant Drew noticed right away. "Is everything all right, Miss Loraine?"

She gave the lad a hug and replied, "Not everything yet, Drew. But they are certainly much better. I'm going to the theatre. Would you like to ride along?"

"Yes ma'am!" he replied excitedly, donning his cap.

Turning to Holmes and me she said, "Mr. Holmes, I thank you for solving the crime. I promise you that I shall continue to resolve the rest of the case. Please let me know your fee at your earliest convenience. I may be temporarily out of work but I do have income properties to draw upon."

Holmes gave a slight bow and stated, "I have already been advised that remuneration for your case will be taken care of by the theatre, Miss Fontaine. Irving is an old friend and was quite grateful to know his star will be returning, unencumbered by threats of violence."

"Well, I shall have to thank him," she replied, "And you, Dr. Watson, thank you for all your efforts and please, take very good care of this excellent wife of yours."

"I shall indeed, Miss Fontaine. She is my treasure," I answered with a smile at my beloved.

Miss Brooke then reached out to shake Holmes hand, "Thank you sir, for allowing me to participate in this exercise. My conclusion was correct then?"

"Yes indeed, Miss Brooke. I trust you will fill in Inspector Lestrade so as to round out his case against Henshaw and secure the release of Dryden?"

"I will, sir. It will be a pleasure," she smiled.

Then I walked her, Miss Fontaine and Drew out to hail a cab. Returning I found Mary and Holmes upstairs engaged in conversation in our old sitting room.

"Holmes," I broke in, "what conclusion was Miss Brooke referring to?"

My friend took a drag from his pipe and replied. "Miss Brooke is an unusually perceptive and persistent officer of the Yard. I had sent her my monograph on observance of family resemblance. She thus confirmed my recognition of Drew as the brother of our client. She could go far in her career."

"Capital!" I exclaimed. "The Yard could use more women in their service." Turning to my wife I enquired, "So, is there a reconciliation in the future of our client and her mother?"

"She will make the attempt John," replied Mary, "The doctor still has her 'taking it easy', as if that were possible for a woman like Lilly, but she implied that she may take a trip to her mother's bedside within the week. She may also take Drew with her after a good long talk."

"Well then," boomed Holmes as he poured drinks for the three of us, "the crime is solved, and the case will be resolved one way or the other very soon."

Handing a glass of wine to Mary and me, he then raised his own, "To you, Mary Watson, for bringing me this excellent little problem and for your part in its resolution."

"Hear, hear!" I agreed and we clinked our glasses and drank our toast.

I then raised my glass and announced, "To my darling wife, for bringing a woman's touch to crime solving!"

After this sip, Mary raised her own glass and spoke quietly but firmly, "To Sherlock Holmes and Dr. John Watson, rescuers of ladies fair!"

With that final swallow, Mary and I excused ourselves to return home. As we walked into the hallway, I realized I had forgotten my cane and stepped back in to retrieve it, whereupon I spied Holmes, looking rather pensively into his desk drawer.

Perceiving my presence he closed the drawer and looked toward me. I nodded and saluted him with my cane. I knew that it was not his seven percent solution he sought in his loneliness, but in that drawer was the picture he kept of another actress. *The* Woman, who had a special meaning for him.

Epilogue

Six weeks later, I found myself in Baker Street. I was returning to my practice after visiting a patient, and decided to drop in at my old lodgings. I discovered Holmes, lounging by the fire, grey plumes of cherry-scented smoke swirling about his head. He languidly puffed away at one of his briarwood pipes, and was scouring through the evening newspapers.

"Watson, dear fellow! Come in, come in! Your old chair awaits you. Pray take a seat and join me for a smoke. I perceive that you have some little time on your hands prior to rejoining your most excellent wife for dinner. Rivano's, I believe?"

I had started to deposit myself in my favourite armchair and found myself startled.

I dropped the remaining few inches with a decided jolt at the mention of the very restaurant where Mary and I had intended to enjoy our evening cuisine.

"Holmes, I never realized how much I miss being taken aback by your pronouncements. What observations led you to your conclusions this time?"

"We have spent a number of years as fellow lodgers, my friend. Certainly you must realize that I would note your habits. Even though married life has rearranged your schedule somewhat, you have easily adjusted. Once again, you are quite predictable.

"On those occasions when I have come by to steal you away from Mary's affections to help me on a case, I have noted that your routine dinner time is six o'clock.

It is the time that allows you to quit your practice, slip into comfortable attire and sit down to a well-prepared meal.

"However, when you and your lovely bride decided to dine out for the evening, you habitually make reservations for seven o'clock. This allows you time to refresh your toilet, change into evening clothes and travel to your destination.

"The fact that it is now quarter past five and you perceived that you had time enough to drop in on your old friend, tells me that dinner is not prepared for six o'clock on this fine evening. Also, that your choice of restaurant is not far from your house."

"All true ..." I answered, smiling at his deductions and the intonation he always used when explaining himself. Rather like a schoolmaster to his student. "But how did you arrive at Rivano's?"

"The criteria, my dear fellow. I am well aware that both you and Mary have a penchant for Italian food, and Rivano's is walking distance from your home, so it fits the time frame. As to the fact that you have chosen an Italian restaurant, I perceive that you have already secreted a packet of bicarbonate of soda within your waistcoat pocket, which you will transfer to your dinner jacket when you change. It is your usual precaution due to your occasional bouts of indigestion after some of the spicier dishes brought to our shores by the sons of Italy."

Chuckling, I congratulated him on the accuracy of his deductions and asked how his work was getting on.

"I have high hopes of busying myself on the morrow, Watson. Inspector Gregson is coming by with a puzzle later this evening, which I hope will be suitable exercise for my wits. But have you seen this? It brings our recent case to a fitting close."

He handed me the *Evening Chronicle* and I immediately took note of the following article under the heading 'Actress Recovers, New Play Scheduled':

Noted actress, Loraine Fontaine, who was recently taken ill under mysterious circumstances, has announced a full recovery. She will return to the stage for the September production of *Ravenswood*, Mr. Herman Merivale's dramatization of Scott's Bride of Lammermoor, produced by Henry Irving at the Lyceum theatre.

The sensational young actress has taken London by storm over the past four years, with charm, wit and the ability to play a variety of parts. Noted for her remarkable talent in all forms of theatre, she is predicted to become one of the great actresses of our time. Ticket sales are expected to be at a premium.

"Well," I responded, "it seems our fair Miss Fontaine is moving along nicely with her life. She is reconciled with her mother and has taken in young Drew. Mary tells me she has also been spending a great deal of social time with Lionel Ferguson. As far as her acting, I believe she has the potential for a great career. What do you think, Holmes?"

Holmes had stood by the mantelpiece and re-stuffed his pipe anew from the Persian slipper as I was reading and making my comments. Now, as he lit his latest taste in tobacco, he looked thoughtful and spoke with a quiet passion.

"Watson, I have observed that 'greatness' is a double-edged sword. For where you find great abilities, great wealth, great fame, even great love, there can be equally great envy, great despair, great ambition and great hatred. It is a sad state of the human condition and I fear that we shall never be rid of it. It has come down to us since the slaying of Abel by Cain. But, we can always hope, Watson. Until that day, however," his mouth twitched, with just a hint of a smile, "it appears there shall always be cases to solve for a private consulting detective."

"And it shall be my honour to continue to record them for the public, so that you will be recognized as such," I replied.

"Touche', Watson, touche'."

Facts Within the Fiction

The year 1890 did see the first Tournament of Roses in Pasadena, California. It was also the year that Scotland Yard moved in to New Scotland Yard. The Bow Street Station Police Strike occurred that year and the National Telephone Company would extend its service into the Woodside Park area in autumn. *Ravenswood*, Mr. Herman Merivale's dramatization of Scott's *Bride of Lammermoor*, was produced by Henry Irving at the Lyceum Theatre in September of 1890.

The North Middlesex Golf Club would be established in 1905. It is only speculation that the land purchases would have begun this early.

St. Albans is home to the National Rose Society and its entrance was much like that described herein.

Catherine Louisa Pirkis authored *The Experiences of Loveday Brooke, Lady Detective* in 1894. There is no mention of Miss Brooke's early training as a detective and it is pure speculation that she began at Scotland Yard and was mentored by Holmes, prior to her joining Ebenezer Dyer's private detective agency.

Hannah Chaplin was the mother of Charlie Chaplin. She became a Music Hall entertainer and used the stage name 'Lily Harley'.

On 16th March, 1885, she gave birth to Sidney John Hill, later Sydney Chaplin. On 22nd June the same year, she married Charles Spencer Chaplin, a fellow Music Hall entertainer. Their son Charles was born in 1889. She gave birth to George Dryden on 31st August 1892 in London, son of music hall entertainer Leo Dryden, but as a result of her adulterous relationship with Dryden, Hannah and Charles Chaplin, separated soon after George's birth.

Lightning Source UK Ltd.
Milton Keynes UK
UKOW042134290612

195223UK00004B/11/P